ORIGINAL PLAYER

Original Player
You Get Out of the Game What You Put In

Copyright © 2020 by John Isom

paperback ISBN: 978-0-578-79631-4
e-book ISBN: 978-0-578-79632-1

Publishing Manager: Christian Eddings

Cover design by DTPerfect.com
Cover photos licensed from DepositPhotos.com

ORIGINAL PLAYER

YOU GET OUT OF THE GAME
WHAT YOU PUT IN

MONTREAL EVANS
AND JOHN ISOM

Part 1

The Beginning

*"You get out the game
what you put in."*

-UNKNOWN

Remember, there's only
envy, cheating, greed, sex, money,
and even murder.

1

I HAD A GOOD RUN back in the day and made some good money selling dope, but that got me ten years in an Arkansas prison.

They call me Big E — short for Evan Barrow — and I was about to get out of prison. While I was down I had gotten in good with these two officers; a muscle-bound nigga named Gee and a thick yellow bone that was tall and tatted named Sunni.

I'd talk to them whenever they were on shift, which was a few times a week. Gee went off and Sunni came on. They were both aware that my time was just about up. The day before I was gonna make my break Gee asked me, "Whatcha gonna do when you touch down this time?'

I paused mid-workout and looked up at him. "Man, I got my mind set on a strip club."

He stared at me for a minute. "Bruh, it's a lotta strip joints in Little Rock. You need to get you something that's gonna make some money."

"Nah man, it's gonna be a hard body strip club, with male strippers, and for women only."

"Man, that's what's up! Let me know what I need to do to put some money behind you when you start out."

"Aight, but you gonna be my right-hand man, too," I told Gee, cranking out pushups.

"That's what's up my guy. But go on an finish getting ya work out on." He straightened up and moved on down the block to finish his rounds.

I turned up my amplified radio, bumping "Caprice Music" by Tum Tum before getting down to knock out my last set of push-ups. There was a light tap on the door. I looked up to see Sunni standing there.

"Why every time I come round you working out?" she asked, some teasing to her voice.

"Well a nigga 'bout to be free, and the women are going to bore me," I shot back. Sunni had been an officer for about half my time here and we'd gotten to know each other real good. She dropped by to talk often and I couldn't help from checking her out every time she walked away. So did everyone else on the block — the men always stepped up when she was around, most tryina holla, some just watching. But we kept it professional. Preferential treatment in the pen doesn't do nobody no good.

"So, where you going back to? Lil Rock?" she asked.

"Yeah, that's my home," I replied.

"And whatchu gonna do so you won't come back?" Sunni and Gee both knew me well enough to want me to get out and stay out. They understood the hardships of life and how I had gotten here, but that didn't mean I had to make mistakes once I got out.

"I'ma own my own business," I told her.

"And what's that gonna be?" she asked, intrigued.

"A strip club."

I'd been working on the idea for a long time, but didn't

discuss it with anyone. Especially since it would be something new in Little Rock that would attract a lot of attention. I didn't need a nigga getting out before me and using my business idea to succeed.

"You not gonna get no money from that!" Sunni said with a snort of laughter.

"Why you say that?" I asked, sitting up and running my eyes up her thick thighs. She looked good in that uniform, even with her hair up in a tight bun and under a cap.

"Because it's strip clubs all ova Lil Rock."

"Not like the one I'm opening. It's gonna be big ma, you'll see, and I'd like you to be at my grand opening."

"Boy please. I'm not coming to see no women strip!" she shot back with an eye roll.

"Now ma, these are gonna be male strippers," I told her.

She glanced at me, quickly checking out my body in the prison issue tank they gave us all. "Now that's how you can get my money," she said before smirking and strutting off.

Anybody could see that we had a thing for each other. But I didn't know too much about her life outside the pen, and didn't want to make a move on her without knowing where her loyalties were.

Before she got off the wing, she came back around and said, "So when you're up and jump'n get at me on da' book and let me know what's up, because me and my girls will be in this real talk."

"I got you mami," I said. She looked good as hell in that uniform and I couldn't even imagine how she'd look on the outside.

"Go on an finish ya workout." She left for the last few hours of her shift.

I had a day left in prison and I didn't have any money to get my business off the ground. I hadn't asked anyone but no one had come forward to offer either. Only my sister Kay and my lil girl wrote letters. Kay didn't wanna bring Babygirl to the pen, and I could understand that, but I only ever got to see pictures of my daughter and was ready to see her face to face.

If I was going to support my family I'd need money to get it jumpin. Going down for the night I thought, *Man, I can't go back to Lil Jon. He gonna want to put in work, and I ain't tryna come back to the pen.*

But Gee had offered to throw some money my way, and I went to sleep thinking of that possibility.

—•—

The last day went by fast. They called my name, pulling me out of my thoughts. I got my stuff and headed out the door. The only things in the brown paper sack they gave me were clothes that didn't fit no more and an old two-way pager that Lil Jon had given me back in the day.

I caught the bus back to the Rock. Getting off back home people was muggin' me like, "Who's this nigga?" I'd been gone ten years so I couldn't blame them. Home looked good. I looked up at the sky and thanked God for bringing me back safely and with a plan.

At the payphone I tried to call Kay at her house, but got no answer. In the last letter to her we'd discussed her picking me up, but she was nowhere to be found. Instead I turned to see an unfamiliar Black SK500 Benz pulling up with black tinted windows. It stopped right next to me and the window on the driver side rolled down. Lil Jon was sat inside.

Oh shit, this nigga again.

"What up my guy?" he asked like he wasn't the whole reason I went to the pen in the first place.

"Not shit, just got back in town," I told him.

"Come get in man." He leaned over and pushed open the passenger side door.

"My sista coming to get me," I replied, not looking at him.

"Bruh, I told her I'd scoop you up."

Did Kay want me going back already? I didn't want to fool with this cat again. I took the fall for him ten years ago and he didn't send me a dime, never called, never came to see me. But I didn't have a choice if Kay wasn't comin to get me. I jumped in the car and he asked did I want to get something to eat.

"Nah, I'm good, just want to go back to my sista's that's all," I said.

"So what's been up with you?" he asked.

"Bro, you was not there for me them ten years and now you want to come back around? Where dey do that at? Let me know," I busted out in anger. Ten years wasn't long enough for me to have patience for him.

He looked at me and said, "Bro, forgive me for not having your back while you were gone. I was looking out for your sister and Babygirl. But I'm not the bad guy. Where are you gonna find guys like me when your Babygirl need school clothes and your sister needs help with bills?" he scolded. Kay hadn't mentioned that he was doin all that for them.

"Thank you for doing that for me," I said, feeling less angry knowing that my fam was taken care of while I was away.

"The respect I got for you is a lifetime. Big E, you still Big Bro, don't forget that. You here now fam so can we get something to eat?"

"I guess we can bro," I replied, but he caught the tone of my voice.

Lil' Jon slowed down at a light and looked over at me. "Why you got an attitude?" he asked. "I'm out here doing you a favor, I been doing your family a favor while you were away, and now you got an attitude."

"Nigga you did *me* a favor?" I exclaimed. "I went away for you! You wouldn't have had to look after my fam if I hadn't taken the fall. And the way you showed up today, I can already tell you planning something, and you need to understand that I'm not going back!"

Lil Jon looked a little ashamed, but he was giving that side eye that I recognized. He was definitely planning something, and I didn't like it.

"I'm not asking you to get involved again bro. Can't lie, it would help me out, I'm short on help now. But you did more than enough for me the first time around. I'm just here to pay you back."

I kept quiet, watching as he drove through the city, gunning it through yellow lights and slowing down for Lil Jon to greet friends and customers. After calling out to a group of fine women, he turned back to me.

"Oh, and I got you some fresh fits too. You gonna look fresh big dog. What do you want to eat?"

"Man, let's get some fish." Prison food wasn't shit and I'd been craving a good fish platter for a while.

"And I got you two females for the night," he added. That was normal. Anyone who got outta the pen usually spent their first night with a woman or two, if they didn't already have one. I just nodded, but all I could think about was Sunni. She wasn't on the block today so I didn't get to say goodbye. But I just wanted to be with her tonight.

"So what're we going to do this time? You need some dope?" he asked me.

"Nah bruh, I'm not with that no more," I told him, and I meant it. I wasn't going back. Not now that I had plans for myself and a future.

"All you gonna do is get a 9 to 5 working for the white man," he said, shaking his head.

"It's better than being in prison. I'd rather be out here with these beautiful sistas," I shot back. It had been a long time since I seen so many beautiful women out walking the streets. Only Sunni and a few women who worked in the cafeteria were what I got to look at every day, until now. There were all types of women out there and I woulda been happy with any of them if it hadn't been for Sunni occupying my mind.

"We gonna talk tonight when you swing by later," Lil Jon said like he was sure he'd convince me to go back to the dope game. I didn't bother answering. There was no point having the same argument over and over again. He'd see when I got my shit straight that I was above that now, and going to do well for myself.

We pulled up to the fish spot. Getting out the car, I noticed two thick white girls walking across the parking lot. The blonde stopped and eyed me, then approached and said, "Hey, what's your name handsome?"

"Big E," I replied with a grin.

"Well Big E, you're looking good," the cute blonde said. Her friend stayed by their car.

"Thank you. If you need a workout partner you should call me," I said.

She laughed at that. "Sure, what's your number?" She pulled out a pink cased Android. I gave her Lil Jon's number. At some point I'd have to stop and pick up a new phone. She headed back to her car, throwing an extra twist to them hips. I just smiled.

As they pulled out the lot, she yelled "I'll get atcha big daddy!"

In my mind I was still looking at the bigger picture of getting this paper to start my club, but it was nice to be recognized by females. As we entered the fish joint we spotted some more females inside. When we came to the counter, the black china doll caught my eye.

"May I help you?" she asked with a killa smile.

I was kind of dazed from her beauty. Lil Jon snapped, bringing me back to earth. She laughed and we ordered a platter of catfish, fries, hush puppies, and coleslaw.

While waiting on our order I made small talk and found out that she was single without kids.

"They call me T-Baby," she told me with that smile again. I asked could I have her number. She gave me a hard time but gave it up, and I told her I'd call her later.

"They call me Big E, by the way," I said, as Lil Jon paid for our food. We headed toward some seats in the corner by the two other women in the spot. As soon as we sat I dug into my fish and fries.

After a few minutes I swallowed and said, "Bro, I was going to talk to you later about putting some stuff together. But I need money to get things started." Lil Jon eyed me.

"How much we talking?" he asked.

"One hundred grand," I replied, starting in on those hush puppies.

"Fuck is you putting together!?" he said real loud. It wasn't every day a nigga asked for that much money, but I knew he probably had it. He'd been running the game for years, long before I went away.

"Bruh, we gonna make that plus some if you let me handle my business."

"We'll see bruh, that's a lot of paper. What you doing that calls for this much paper?" he asked.

"It's for the women, fam." I told him.

"Aww. Okay, now we getting somewhere," he said, rubbing his hands together. "Tell me more."

"Well, it's gonna be a strip club."

He stopped eating and stared at me. "A strip club! Man

I'm not investing my money in no shit like that!"

"Bruh, this is gonna be big," I insisted.

"Nigga, do you know how many strip joints there are out here?"

"Yeah, but this one is different."

"Explain."

"The name is gonna be 'Hard Body Strippers.'"

"Fam come on, so the females gonna have hard bodies, man get the fuck outta here with that BS!" he said. I had to stop myself laughing at his reaction.

"Now nigga, it's gonna be male strippers. Hell, ever since I've been home, women look at me and want to jump in my lap left and right," I said. He couldn't argue with that. "This will jump because women don't have shit like that down here," I continued, looking over to the sexy females eating a few tables down.

"Can I ask ya'll a question?" I called, and they turned to look at me before coming over cautiously.

The shorter, tatted female who looked like Jada Fire the pornstar eyed me up. I introduced myself and my homeboy Lil Jon. She told me her name was Rose, and the other lil chocolate female's name was Rhonda. She was just as thick as her homegirl. They kind of looked alike as far as dressing, but Rhonda looked like a darker Lisa Ray.

"Ma, if it was a male strip club out here, would ya'll come?" I asked Rose.

"Hell yeah we'd come!" she said excitedly. "When is it coming here? Where at?" she asked.

"You'll know sooner than later, and thank you," I said. They headed back to their table.

"Man, that's only two females!" Lil Jon said, but he was starting to look convinced. We finished eating and got up to leave. I nodded to T-Baby on the way out, reminding her to look for my call.

The heat rushed us as soon as we got outside. Just before we got in the car I realized that Rose and Rhonda was coming out walking toward us.

"Hey Big E, hold on a second," Rose said.

"What's good sexy?" I asked.

"Do ya'll got a girl?" Females were a lot more straight-forward now. Back in the day I woulda had to chase after them, but they were flocking to me now.

"Nah, we single, and plus I just got back in town. I've been gone ten years," I told her.

"So you was locked up?" she asked, and I just nodded. "Well we gonna need ya'lls number so we can link up."

They gave Lil Jon both numbers and he flirted for a minute.

"Well we'll be seeing ya'll around, ya'll take care," I said, and got in the car. We headed toward Kay's house.

We pulled up on her street and it was a long line of cars out front, but I didn't think they were for me. Kay was always social and had so many friends I couldn't keep count. I gathered my stuff and got out. Before I closed the door, Lil Jon said, "I'ma catch you later and we gonna put that into play fam, you be good bro."

I closed the door and headed for the house. Approaching the door, I knocked a couple of times and waited. My big sister Kay appeared.

"Bro! What's up!? It's good to see you back home with us today," she said, giving me a big hug.

"Man, I called you to pick me up and you send that nigga Lil Jon!" I said angrily.

"Boy hush! That was your best friend. I know he did you wrong letting you take the fall for him, but we made amends. Now come on in, you letting the flies in!" she said with a laugh. I let it go, but knew I'd have to talk to her later and explain that I didn't plan on knowing him for too long if he was going to try to drag me back into the game.

People jumped out as I entered the house and it threw me off. I stumbled against the wall and got to looking at all my family and friends.

"Good to see you back Big E," everyone said.

"Thank you."

Someone jumped on my back. When I shook them off and turned around it was my Babygirl.

"Hi daddy! How you been?" she asked, giving me a tight hug and kissing my cheek. "I missed you daddy and love you," she said. We'd only gotten to talk through letters, but I knew my little girl right away. She'd been born right after I went away and had been living with Kay since her mom disappeared years ago.

When I first went away me and Kay had talked about if it would be good for her to see me locked up or not, and decided against it. Kay made sure Babygirl understood that I'd made mistakes, but was still a good man. I got to know her through her letters and sometimes phone calls. Kay was good about sending me pictures, but seeing my baby in person brought tears to my eyes.

"I love you too," I told her. She showed me around the house as I greeted people, and Kay interrupted to let me know she'd made a buncha food. We all had a good time that night, catching up and hanging out. I slept really good for the first time in ten years in a queen sized bed, with my family close by.

—•—

I woke up the next morning and called Gee first thing. He answered on the second ring.

"What's good homie?" I said. I'd given him my number

the day before getting out, so he knew it was me.

"I see you didn't forget about me."

"Man, come on you my righthand, how can I forget about you? So what's up, are we gonna put that down?" I asked.

"I got you bro," he said.

"Alright. I need you to do me a favor — first, you know if Sunni got a man?" It wasn't something me and her ever talked about, but I was curious. She didn't act like she had a man but a lot of women didn't. I wasn't going to pursue her unless I knew I had a straight shot.

"Man, I don't think so, but you know she's pretty private. Never heard her mention a man though so I think you've got a chance. You thinking about going for it now that you're out?"

"Hell yeah. Can you get at Sunni and tell her to give me a call?" I asked. He had her number from work and taking each other's shifts sometimes.

"Okay, I'll get back with you," he said, and we hung up.

Sunni had been on my mind all yesterday and this morning. I passed up the females Lil Jon had for me because all I really wanted was to spend some time with Sunni and get to know her better. I wasn't looking for just a hook up — I wanted something real, and I knew the moment I met Sunni that we had a vibe. I was just hoping she felt the same way.

A little while later the phone started ringing.

"Hello," I answered.

"Yes, is this Big E?" a feminine voice asked.

"Dis me, who dis?"

"This Sunni, I'm glad to hear from you!" she said, and I could tell she meant it.

I asked her what she was doing right now. She replied, "I'm in my bed thinking about you now, and looking at TV. I hope you was going to get at a sista," she said, and continued, "You know I wanted to get at you when you was locked up. You was always on my mind. Then I'd go home at night and think about you some more." She sounded nervous and excited.

"You did, huh? Well when I was in that cell, I'd look at you all the time and told myself that I was going to have you. Now look at me — I got a queen in my life, and I'm happy to have you," I told her. "So, what you got planned for the day?"

"I'd like to take you to lunch and give you some of this time I've been wanting to give you for the last ten years," she replied. "But I have to be honest E, I'm not looking for a man who's going to be back inside in a few months."

"Well my head is on right this time, and I want to get this club jumping, and I don't wanna get involved with dope again. I'm going to do my shit right. And I need you by my side to keep me straight. We gonna come up together. I want the whole hundred yards, big family, big house, nice rides, that's what I'm pushing for this time. This is my goal."

It was a lot to tell a woman right off but I needed Sunni to understand I was serious about her and about getting my life together. I'd already lost ten years, and I didn't want to waste any more time.

She listened to everything I said and seemed to appreciate the honesty. I'd been wanting to say that to her for a while, but not while I was on the inside.

"We will see," she said sweetly. "You're home now and I'm here with you. I'm going to help you do it right, too. But I'm happy you're home. Now I can spend time with you on the outside. So what'd you do last night?" she asked.

"I kicked it with my family. We ate and danced and I caught up with my daughter. She was so happy to see me, I was happy to see her too. Last time I saw her she was a baby, but she's a young sweetheart, and I'm home to be there for her now," I said. "What'd you do last night?" I asked her.

"Kicked it with my homegirls. We went out to have drinks."

"That was all? Ya nigga wasn't around?"

"I don't have a nigga. Why, are you speaking up?" she asked with a playful attitude.

"Maybe I was hoping you'd give me a chance," I said.

"Maybe Big E, you gotta do right first," she replied seriously.

"I mean we could have some real fun together," I told her.

"Well, I was hoping to see you today if that's okay?"

"Yeah that's cool ma. I'd like to spend the day with you," I said.

"I don't want to stop you from doing your business today."

"It's cool ma, what time you talking?" I asked.

"About 1:30PM," she said.

"Okay, I'll see you then."

By this time Kay was up and came into the guest bedroom where I was staying.

"What's up bro? You hungry?" she asked. I nodded. She told me she was making eggs, pancakes, fried ham and hash browns. I asked her was she working and she replied, "Yeah, why you ask me that?"

"Because I talked to Lil Jon and he said he helped you with some bills and with Babygirl's school clothes," I said.

"At the time I wasn't working and we needed some help. That is my bro too, don't forget that!" she said with an attitude. Then the doorbell rang.

I got up to check on it while Kay cooked. Speak of the devil, it was Lil Jon, and he handed me a big bag that looked like it came from the mall. "This is for you big bro."

I took a look in the bag and it was the clothes he bought for me. "Appreciate it bro. When I'm back on my feet, I'ma look out," I promised.

"Man, come on with that. You my brotha, and when you get dressed and shaved, I need you to ride with me," he said.

I nodded, but didn't like feeling like I owed him. Lil Jon and me had grown up together, but he went a different direction than me and had gotten deeper in the game. I was worried he'd try to take advantage, and buying me shit while I couldn't pay him back would put me in that spot.

I said I'd be ready in an hour and shut the door, heading to where my daughter was sleeping. I gave her a kiss and let her know Ima give her the world, and she can have whatever she wants. I went to the kitchen and made me a quick egg, ham and hash brown sandwich. Then went to change into the fit Lil Jon got me. As much as I didn't like owing him it felt good to be wearing something other than a uniform. I couldn't remember the last time I had new clothes, clothes that fit well, and looking in the mirror I knew I looked good.

I come back to the kitchen dressed and shaved after thirty minutes, sat and ate my sandwich.

"This is good Kay," I told her with my mouth full. When I was done I gave her a quick kiss and told her I'd see her later.

"Hey," she said before I could go out the door. "Don't go getting mixed up in any of that dope this, aight? I don't want you going back already."

"You know me better than that," I said. "I'm done with all that. Lil Jon just wants to make amends, and I already told him I'm not helping him out with that game anymore."

"You need to be here for me and your daughter Big E. We need you."

"I know. I'm not going anywhere sis." I gave her a hug and locked the door behind me.

Jon was waiting in the driveway with the windows rolled down, bumpin a new speaker set in the back. We headed out and I asked him did he have anything in the car.

"We clean," he said. "I don't handle the business myself these days. Unless it's a special client. Some of the other boys run product for me." He fired down on a blunt and asked if I wanted a hit. I shook my head.

"I want this money."

"I'ma have you right tonight, but here go five grand for your pockets," he said, tossing it in my lap.

"Where we going?" I asked.

"Just sit back and ride bro," he told me. We were somewhere in North Little Rock and pulled in front of this big ass house. We parked and got out and went to the door. He put a key in the lock and opened it.

"Is this your spot?" I asked, surprised. He'd been doing well when I went away but nothing like this.

"One of them," he said, and showed me in. I followed him into the living room and took a seat and turned on the flatscreen. He went to the back room and a minute later hollered my name. I went to see what the nigga screamin for. I opened the door and there was three thick ass white girls.

"Man, who are these women?" I asked.

"Just business partners is all," he said.

"What's ya'lls name?" I asked. They were all lookin me up and down.

"Ms. D, Tana, and Kim," Lil Jon said, pointing to each one.

Ms. D was thick like a sista and Lil Jon knew that's what I liked. He was grinning at me.

"Which one you want?" I asked again.

"It's business with them fam," he said, greeting the women one by one. "They help me run shit and keep it all organized."

He then gave me a set of car keys and said, "That's for you fam, in the garage."

I went through the kitchen to the garage and seen a red 745 BMW.

"That's me?" I asked as Lil Jon came up behind me.

"Yeah, I got you big bro," he said.

I smiled and asked Ms. D did she wanna take a ride. She said yeah and went to get dressed. I waited in the car; she came back minutes later ready to ride. I cranked the car up and backed out the garage. We drove off bumping that "All I do is Win" by DJ Khaled.

"So you're the famous Big E," she said with a smirk. I knew right away I was in trouble, but I found myself drawn to her.

"Don't believe everything you hear," I told her.

I asked her what she did for a living and she replied, "I have my own business."

"And what is that?" I asked.

"To keep people like your bro out here eating in these streets," she said.

"Okay." I could respect that. She seemed smart and was probably keeping enough of a distance that if anything went down, there wouldn't be consequences for her.

"Do you like the car?" she asked.

"Yeah I do. Would it be okay if I got your number from my bro?" I asked her.

"Yeah, that's cool, but you could just get it from me," she said. I told her to write it down for me, because I didn't have a phone yet, and was on my way to Cricket right now to get one real quick. We stopped by the store and I ended up buying me a flip phone. Heading back to the car, I noticed how good Ms. D looked in my BMW. I got in and told her to key her number in.

We pulled back up to the house and I parked behind Lil Jon's black Benz SL 500. We got out and went into this house. I went to the living room and watched some TV until Lil Jon came out from the back. I decided to call Gee and check in.

"What's good fam?" he answered.

"Not shit bro, but how much you got right now?" I asked him.

"Man, I got $4,500 now," he replied.

"Look, we don't have shit right now. So my brotha told me he was gonna front me the money tonight," I told him.

"That's what's up, I'm gonna let this job go then," he said.

"Nah, don't do it until we get this money. But listen — we need to be careful. Lil Jon is the guy I was working with when I got caught."

"Well shit. You sure this is a good idea E?" I could hear that Gee was a little nervous, but we'd known each other long enough that he would trust me.

"It is. He knows now he can't get me back in the game. This is all about building up my business, and I'll pay him back as soon as we start making this money. We won't be on the hook with him for long."

"Okay," he said, and I disconnect the call and looked at my phone. It was bout that time to link up with Sunni. I gave her a call. She answered right away.

"Hello...who dis?" she asked.

"Dis E, I went and got me a cell phone today," I told her.

"Cool, where you at now?" she asked.

"I'm in North Little Rock. Meet me at John Barrow," I told her.

"Where we going?"

"To this BBQ joint. They got some damn good BBQ too," I told her.

"Okay, I'm on my way there now," she said, and we disconnected our call. I went and told bro I'd catch him later tonight, and told Ms. D to be looking for my call.

As I headed out the door the heat overtook me immediately. I rushed to my car and got in to crank up the A/C. I pulled off bumping some Cash Money. I thought to myself, *Man, I'ma have this city on lock.*

When I got to John Barrow and pulled up to Jim's BBQ,

I saw Sunni's Q50 Infinity parked out front. She got out and I don't know how, but when she seen the BMW she knew it was me. She looked so good to me. I gave her a hug and kissed her forehead. We went in and headed for the counter to place an order.

"May I take ya order?" this barrel-chested brother asked.

I ordered ribs, beans, coleslaw, and a large coke. Sunni got some polish sausages with beans and coleslaw and a water.

"So how many women you get last night?" she asked.

"Only one," I told her.

"I don't believe you," she said.

"Why you don't believe me, I'm forreal!" I told her. "Listen, I'm not messing around anymore bae. I'm looking for a partner, not someone playing games."

She smiled, but didn't say anything to that. Instead she asked, "And who's car is that?"

I considered her for a second wondering if she was avoiding a conversation about what we were looking for in a relationship.

"Well, it's mine. Do you like it?" I asked instead of pursuing the other topic. Maybe she just needed me to prove that I was serious about her.

"Yes I do, but I hope you not selling dope no more? Because it kinda looking like it."

"I just got out, why would I do that again? I just got good friends that owe me favors," I insisted.

"I want you to stay out, E!"

"I am, and I want you to run this business with me," I told her, but our food came, interrupting the conversation. She thanked me but still looked distrustful.

"You don't have to work tonight, can I come spend time with you?" I asked.

"If you want to."

"Do I need to get a room?" I asked her. If she needed space before she made any decisions about us, I could give her that.

"Nah, you can come ova to my place if you want," she said with a smile. While we were eating my phone started ringing. I pulled it out and saw that it was my man Gee.

"What up my guy?" I asked.

"Well I got this guy that got 150 tables for sale," he said.

"And how much he want?" I asked.

"800 for all."

"Where you at?"

"In the Bluff. Where are we gonna put them at?" he asked.

"My family has a place for now," I told him, thinking that Kay would be cool keeping them in her garage.

"Okay, I'll let him know we'll take them."

"I'll get up with you. Oh, and I'm here with ya coworker," I told him.

"Tell her I said what's up, and ya'll be good Big E," he said and hung up.

"Since you done, do you want to go ova my sister's for a minute?" I asked as I wiped my hands on some napkins.

"We can. I'm with you today," Sunni answered with a smile.

I paid for our food and we headed for the door.

"Where'd you get all that money, E? You just got out," she said with an attitude when we reached the cars. "I guess your homeboy gave you that too?"

"Yes he did. Mami, I got this, just know that. Now give me a kiss cry baby." I said. I got in my car and she followed me to my sister's house.

We pulled up and parked at Kay's, got out and went to the door. I rang the bell and Babygirl answered.

2

"DAD, WHAT'S UP? WHERE YOU been?' Babygirl asked.

"Daddy had to get us a ride," I told her. She looked out the window to where Sunni was pulling up.

"That red car is yours?" she asked.

"Yes, and it'll be yours when you get older," I told her.

"Dad, who's that woman?"

"She's my friend, her name is Sunni. Can you say hi to her?" I asked as Sunni came up next to me and smiled at Babygirl.

"Hi Sunni, my name is Babygirl. Do you like my dad?" my girl asked.

"Yes I do," Sunni said.

"Babygirl, leave her alone," I laughed, motioning her back in the house.

"It's okay. I love talking to kids. So how old are you?" she asked Babygirl.

"Nine. Do you have any kids?"

"No, but I do want them one day," Sunni replied, and glanced at me when she said that.

"Here comes my big sister," I said as Kay rounded the corner.

"Babygirl, who you let in my house!" she yelled.

"My dad and his woman friend Sunni," Babygirl answered, walking further into the house.

"Oh my god, how're you? I'm Kay," sis said, grinning big. I'd told her that there was a woman I was interested in when I was locked up, but I'd never told her Sunni's name or much about her. At the time it seemed like too much to hope for that I might actually have a shot with her. And now, here she was by my side, meeting my family.

"How're you, Ms. Kay?" Sunni asked.

"Well I'm happy Big E's out and hope he stays out this time," Kay said with an attitude. I rolled my eyes.

"I do too girl!"

"My dad got us a new car!" Babygirl interrupted and Kay looked out the window.

"Where'd you get that, Lil Jon?" she asked.

"Yeah, it's a BMW," I said.

"Come on man, you just got out!" I could tell she was jealous, and probably a little distrustful as well. Me, her and Lil Jon grew up together as family, but that didn't mean his mistakes and bad influence would fly.

"Man, I needed my own wheels, I'm a big dude," I said. "Plus you know he owe me."

"I like it, but if you go back to selling dope, I ain't fuckin with you this time, for real!" Kay said.

"My neither," Sunni agreed. I was definitely outnumbered. Even Babygirl was standing there with her arms crossed and looking at me with an attitude. Seeing Sunni fit in so well right off just confirmed that I had strong feelings for her.

"Well Babygirl and I are going to Kids Play. Do ya'll want to join us?" Kay asked, grabbing her purse.

"We good. We about to head to Sunni's house for the night, that okay?"

Kay nodded, giving me a knowing look.

"Do you need some money?" she asked.

"Nah, I'm good," I said.

"Well, ya'll have a good night."

"Babygirl, come give me some loving," I said, and she gave Sunni a hug too. She went out the door. We went into the dining room to watch some TV and rest off some of that BBQ from earlier. I told her to give me a kiss.

"I've been waiting on this all day!" she purred, leaning in.

"Me too."

She pressed herself against me and said, "When you was locked down, I would come round when you worked out and dream about sucking that dick and riding the shit outta you!"

Damn. My girl got right to the point.

"So that's what you want to do to me?" I asked, stroking her waist.

"Yes." She sounded out of breath, almost moaning. Years of tension was finally coming to a head.

"When we get to your place, I'ma let you get what you've been yearning for," I tell her, kissing up and down her neck. I felt her shiver.

"I'm going to see what you talking about, bae," she said, pressing those curves against me even tighter.

"You gonna enjoy it when I get you to that room. Then we can go half on a baby. I want you to know when my club jump off, I don't want you working at that place no more," I said, pulling back and looking her in the eye so she'd know how serious I was.

"Okay, Big E. I hear you."

"I'm gonna put you in a bigger house," I told her. "My brother spotting me the money and Gee got my tables, so things are looking up right now. I just need you to give me some time for everything to come together."

"You forreal, huh?" she asked, sitting up and looking at me seriously. In the pen I'd never really told her my plan for coming up when I got out, but now that I knew she wasn't just playing, I was willing to let her in on it all.

"Bae, I'm not looking back now, real talk. I'm staying here with you and spending this money. And if this don't work, I got more business plans," I said. I looked at the time and it was 6PM. "Well, can we go get a bottle and head to your place? Besides, I gotta get me some clothes to wear for the night and tomorrow," I said, standing.

She gathered her things and I went to pack me an overnight bag before heading to the door. I locked up and went to her car, and when I got in she was playing "Half on a Baby," by R. Kelly. She smiled at me and pulled off, headed toward the liquor store to get us something to drink.

—•—

As we pulled into her driveway I said, "Damn, you got a nice home."

Sunni and I talked a lot when I was in the pen, but not so much about the outside. She didn't want me to miss what I couldn't have, and I didn't want to pry into her life, not knowing if she had a man or family.

"Thank you," she replied.

I grabbed my stuff and she carried the liquor toward the house. As she walked up to the door I checked the area to see if there were any signs of a man in her life. Nothing stood out, which was good.

She opened the door and it was even nicer on the inside. Everything was in its place, and the rooms were big but felt comfortable and like home. She showed me to her bedroom where I put my bags and went back to the living room, where she was drinking this cognac called Twenty Grand. I sat beside her and she handed me a cup of brown liquor on ice.

A quick look around the room told me that everything in here belonged to her; no signs that she was sharing this space with anyone.

"Thanks ma." My phone started to buzz as we were relaxing. I took it out and looked at the screen to see Lil Jon's number.

"What's good bro?" I answered.

"Where you at?"

"In Dumas for the night."

"When you coming back?" he asked.

"Tomorrow."

"I'm gonna make this play than you can do your thang," he said.

"Ms. D got my number now okay? Tell her to get at me tomorrow," I said before hanging up.

I got up and looked at the family photos she had around, and thought, *She's gonna be my wife one day.*

We started to get tipsy and play music. I pulled her to me while she was swaying her thick hips to R. Kelly's "Yellow Light" mix.

"Man, I want you for myself," I told her, tugging a little on her long dark hair.

"You got me, E," she said tipsy like.

"I don't want you with nobody but me," I told her, and she laughed. "And don't forget, I've not had sex in ten years," I added, and she kissed me deeply. I was feeling so good I began to undress her slowly, kissing on every inch of her body that I exposed. It felt good to be her man, in a home that could be our home someday soon.

Finally getting her naked, I carried her to the bedroom and laid her down softly. I looked in her eyes and asked," Do you really want this?" giving her one last out. If we were gonna do this, I was going all in.

She nodded really sexy like.

"It's been a long time, but you here to show me," I said, running my hand down her waist.

"Give it to me daddy!" she said with a deep groan as I continued to kiss on her body, nipping at her neck and sucking on one of those 34D breasts with dark caramel colored nipples. Her body tasted so sweet to me and I was already hard for her. I kissed my way down to that pretty shaved pussy.

She gasped deep in her throat and arched her body off the bed. I lifted both her thighs and kissed my way to her pretty French manicured toes. I popped one of her toes in my mouth and she thrashed around, moaning. I made my way back up to that pussy, sucking on that pussy and letting her cream all over my lips. I licked her cream from my mouth.

"Come fuck me daddy!" she begged.

I stripped in a matter of seconds and she slid to her knees, grabbing my monstrous dick in her soft hands, drawing a groan from me. She stroked me and finally wrapped her lips around my head. Pulling back she said, "Damn! You're big but I'ma handle this."

She stretched her mouth and swallowed my dick whole. After a sloppy but good hand job she crawled back up the bed and I laid down beside her, pulling her on top of me. This way she could have control and I could watch that gorgeous body.

She gripped my manhood and positioned it at her entrance and slid down me taking her time because I knew by the look on her face I was stretching her wide.

"Damn girl! That pussy tight!" I groaned. She slid back up real slow and dropped all the way on it, drawing a groan from me as she gasped for air. She came instantly but she kept on riding me as I gripped that thick, yellow ass. She rode for a minute longer and came two more times before I told her to switch to doggy style.

When she got up on all fours, I got behind her and slid back into her love tunnel. Her pussy was getting better and better. It was worth the wait.

"Fuck me daddy!" she cried out, and I pounded into her pussy until I felt my balls draw up.

"I'm about to cum bae!" I told her, taking a fistful of her hair.

"Me too!" she said, and we came together.

Through it all me and her were in love. We fell out on the bed as my phone rang in my pants pocket on the floor. I got up to get it and pulled it out to see Ms. D's number on my screen.

"What's good?" I answered, out of breath.

"Man, you got to get back! Your brotha killed a dude tryna rob him!" she said, sounding panicked. "They took all the dope and money!" she said, catching her breath.

This is going to fuck with what I got going on, was my first thought. But someone needed to handle Lil Jon's shit, and it was obvious that Ms. D wasn't in the right mindset.

"I'm not in the city right now, but I'll be back first thing in the morning," I told her. "He's going in no matter what so it doesn't matter if I'm there tonight or not. Just lock down his place and let him know I'll handle this." I disconnected the call so I could think.

"Shit," I said out loud.

"What's up bae?" Sunni asked, propping herself up.

"Man, my brotha just killed some cat tryna rob him. Fuck! That's going to stop my business. Man, it's always something!" I groaned.

We laid back down Sunni rubbed my back, trying to relieve some of the tension I was feeling. But I just kept thinking that maybe it was all too good to be true.

Two days out and things were already going so good. I had Gee on my side, had the chance to get the money and start this business, and had a beautiful woman who was falling asleep beside me. I couldn't mess it up this time.

I tried to sleep with Sunni curled up next to me naked. Starting tomorrow there would be a whole lot more to take care of. But maybe I could use it to my advantage.

I cuddled her until I was too tired to think anymore.

—•—

The next morning, Sunni got up and cooked breakfast while I took a shower. I knew from her wet hair and long t-shirt she'd already showered and just didn't want to wake me.

I went into the kitchen and she was making me some eggs, bacon, and toast. I sat down and she said, "Bae, why didn't you get any sleep last night? It seems like there's a whole lot more going on than just your brother getting in trouble."

"The play I put down is gone!" I said, frustrated again at the thought of getting stuck. "Lil Jon was supposed to be a major investor for me. He was going to front me the cash to get started, and instead he got his dumb ass locked up, right where I was these last ten years."

"Don't give up," she insisted, passing me a plate. I just shook my head.

"It's going to take a whole lot to fix his shit and stay on top of mine, too. I can't be wasting my time on his mistakes. Lil Jon might not want to get out of the dope game, but I'm not tryna live that life anymore."

When I finished eating we went to get dressed and I made

a quick call to Gee. He finally answered at 8AM.

"Man, it's over with, my guy gunned a nigga down last night," I told him. "What we gonna do now?"

Gee was silent for a minute. "I'ma figure something out, give me a minute," he said, and we hung up.

"Bae, are you ready to go?" I yelled.

"Yes!" Sunni yelled back.

I gathered my stuff and we headed out. She locked the door behind us. Leaving Dumas, I told her swing by my sister's so I could get my car. She asked could she ride with me and I told her no, that I'd have to link up with her later.

"I'm going to handle some stuff and call you after," I told her.

"Listen E," she said, turning to give me a serious look, "you need to keep your head on straight. You just got out. Don't go lookin for trouble, they'll be right back on you if they think you're connected with this nigga."

I assured her that I wasn't going to jump on anything that would send a nigga back to the pen. After a nice little ride, we finally pulled up to my sister's, and I kissed her goodbye. She pulled off. I walked into the house and yelled for my daughter and sister. No one answered.

"Nobody home," I said to myself. I went to my room and put my bag on the bed and called Ms. D, with my phone on one bar. I sat down and plugged it up for a minute. She finally answered.

"Are you home now?" she asked. She sounded worried but tired.

"Yeah, and I'm about to head your way now," I said, getting my shit together.

I headed out of the house, locking up first. I jumped in the car my lil brother had bought me and smashed out to North Little Rock, keeping the radio off so I could think while driving.

—•—

After making it to North Little Rock I pulled up to my brother's house and parked in the garage. I went in the house through the garage door and saw Ms. D sitting in the kitchen.

"What's up Big E?" she asked.

"Not shit. What went down with him?" I asked her.

"Some guy tried to rob him, so Lil Jon shot and killed him. Didn't even think twice about all this we built, and that was my guy too. We were getting money together!" she said, shaking her head.

"So where is the car at?" I asked. "Where's all the shit he had on him?"

"The police got everything!"

I sat down next to her. "When are you going to see him?"

"I'ma go check on him tomorrow."

"Cool," I replied, making myself as comfortable as possible. Lil Jon had a nice place, but he definitely went a little overboard. If the police came lookin here for anything it would be obvious that he wasn't making money any decent type of way.

"I ain't got no money or dope," Ms. D said, sounding stressed. "I don't got no other job. How am I supposed to get that money now?"

I reached out and took her hand. It was small in mine, and soft. "I know. He was supposed to help me get this business off the ground. I feel you. Lil Jon can be selfish as hell sometimes."

"What business was that?" D asked.

I hesitated, not sure how many people I wanted to know about my plans. Especially a woman I had only met the other day who was involved with my lil bro, someone I went to hell and back for, who was paying for it now.

But when it came down to it, the dream I had needed a support system to succeed. And if Ms. D was all that Lil Jon said she was, she was a large part of why his business had succeeded and grown as fast as it did while I was away.

"I was going to open up my own strip club," I told her, letting go of her hand. Ms. D laughed.

"Boy, it's strip clubs up and down Jackson Street. It ain't no money in that."

"This one I'm opening will."

Ms. D considered me with narrowed eyes. "Well, if I had the money, I'd see what you're working with," she said. "You seem like a man who knows what he's going after."

"I am," I told her. "I had ten years to think about what I wanted to do when I got out. How I'm gonna make that money for my family. I've thought of everything, and nothing gonna stop me," I said. "Not even Lil Jon. I was going to do this without him, and I can still do it without him."

Ms. D was frowning as she looked at me and I knew she was weighing the pros and cons of getting involved. She may be stressed out now, but she was a smart woman, that was obvious.

"You'll bounce back and when you do, give me a call," I told her. "The kind of place I'm lookin to start would be right up your alley."

Ms. D grinned as she finally put together the pieces of my plan and what would make my place stand out.

"Shit, I got some freaky ass homegirls got that money out the ass!" she said. Then it hit me — that me and my guy Gee could make house calls to save toward opening up the club. It would take a while and I hadn't been planning on doing the work myself, but I was willing to do anything to get this shit up and running.

So I let Ms. D know to get at her homegirls and let them

know we'll do house calls, but we ain't fucking with drugs. Just want money to get our shit started.

"You have my number," I told her. "If you hear that anyone wants some entertainment of a certain kind, you know how to reach me."

She asked, "When?" and I told her, "Give me a week and I'll be ready. I need some business cards as well to advertise what I do."

"Well I'll get back with you tomorrow," she said. "I can help you with some of that. I know people and I been running shit since I was in school."

"Oh, let em know we do birthdays and all special requests is extra," I told her as I stood. I kissed her on the forehead and headed out the house. Outside, it was starting to heat up and it was only 9:48 AM. As I was getting in my car, my phone rang. It was Gee again.

"I was bout to call you. What's good my righthand man?" I asked, in a better mood now that I had a plan going.

"I got them tables and can't get my money back," he said.

"Gee, we good," I told him.

"Let me know something," he said.

"Aight, meet me at the gym then so we can get our workout on. We gonna need it."

He agreed and hung up. I got in the car, fired it up and cranked up that "The World is Mine," by Ice Cube, and headed toward the gym. While driving I called Sunni.

She answered with "Nigga, what's up with you!?"

"How'd you figure it was me?" I asked.

"Duh, I got you keyed in my phone."

"Man, you can tell I've been gone for a minute," I said.

"But what did you come up with bae?" she asked.

"You'll be happy," I told her.

All of a sudden it sounded like she was talking to someone

on the other end, but muffling the conversation so I couldn't hear what they were saying or make out who it was. My grip tightened on the steering wheel.

"Where you at?" I asked loudly.

Sunni got back on the line. "Oh I'm just out with my girls. We're getting our nails done. Gotta look tight for my man," she flirted. It sounded like a little much to me but I let it go.

"Come on bae, what's up?" she begged. "Tell me what you planning."

"Well, I stopped by one of bro's spots and his friend Ms. D was there. She told me she was broke and didn't have any dope, which was what Lil Jon was going to use to get me that money. But she had some friends that got paper out the ass. You know me being a black man, I'ma put something together," I told her. "Me and Gee going to do some house calls to save up for the club, if you feel what I'm saying."

"Yes I do," she replied, sounding proud.

"Right now, I'm on my way to the gym to meet Gee."

"Will I see you tonight?" she asked.

"Yeah, I'ma bring Babygirl tonight, but I'm pulling up at the gym. So I'ma have to get back at you later."

She gave me her love before I hung up. I pulled up to see Gee waiting on me. I parked and got out.

"What up Gee?" I asked.

"Man, you need to let me know what's up," he said, agitated.

"Bruh, we in there. We straight now let's go get this money," I told him, and we walked into the gym.

"When we done here, we'll get a bite to eat," I added. "Right now you need to work off that stress. I told you I was gonna take care of all this."

While working out, I told him we gotta get it in for the ladies. He raised his eyebrows.

"We getting started without having a building or any-thing?" he asked.

"Man, it'll be like advertising. Lure them in and then when we do have a spot they'll be flocking to it. But for now we can make that money doing house calls."

Gee considered this. "Alright. I think that could work. Just hit me up with a time and place and I'm in. When we getting started?"

"As soon as my bro's business partner sends me some names and numbers. Not gonna lie, I'm not exactly happy that he got put away, but it's working out for us now. Having Ms. D on our side will definitely make this a successful business."

We went hard for about three hours and headed toward the locker room to freshen up. I put on a pair of gym shorts under my pants and extra boxers in the car, t-shirt too. We headed out for a bite to eat.

Walking outside, the air was dry as hell. We got in our rides and I headed toward the nearest Subway. After about fifteen minutes of driving we pulled up at and beat the heat in the store. I approached the counter to see a fine ass Puerto Rican female. Really slim, olive skin complexion, and very beauti-ful. We ordered sweet onion chicken teriyaki sandwiches on Italian herbs and cheese and then sat down to eat and discuss the plans.

"So, what's the game plan?" Gee asked with his mouth full.

"We are going to be making house calls until we can come up with the money to open the club. D has homegirls with the cake roll. So, if you want to let that job go now you can, because we're bout to get shit jumping," I told him.

By the time I finished telling Gee everything, he was okay with it and had a big smile plastered on his face. "E, you put this together like you said," Gee said, slapping me on the back.

"I told you bruh, I'm not going back to selling dope, and I'm not going back to prison. We are going to be good business partners. I have some more shit regarding money I'ma run by you later on. You'll see," I told him.

"Well I'ma get up outta here, get at me tomorrow." He stood up.

"Come by my sister's tomorrow, I'll text you the address," I told him, and we headed our separate ways.

I started out toward Kay's thinking about everything that was about to take place. When I pulled up, I noticed some girls come down the street toward me. I leaned up on the door of my BMW and cranked up the stereo bumping that "Whatever You Like," by T.I with them fifteen-inch woofers rattling the trunk. Might as well start advertising my business right away.

"What's up with ya'll?" I yelled out. I wanted to approach them, but I was careful not to scare them because I'm a big dude. "They call me Big E," I said, introducing myself as they got closer.

"My name is Bobbi, and this is Stacey, Tammy, and London," the thick white girl with a pixie haircut and tattoos said, introducing herself and her friends.

"How old are ya'll?" I asked.

"Stacey's twenty-three, Tammy's twenty-four, and me and London are twenty-seven," she said.

Okay, I thought, *these are women.*

"So, what kinda job you got to have a nice car like that?" Bobbi asked, walking around the BMW and eyeing it up.

"I'm a male stripper," I told her.

"For real?" she asked, eyes snapping up.

"Yes, I am."

I definitely had their attention.

"So, what're you doing tonight?"

"About what time?"

"9:30. You can come by. Here are our numbers. Give us a call," the young mixed chick Stacey said.

They gave me their numbers one by one.

"We have to get our smoke and drank on before you swing by because it's Bobbi's b-day today," Stacey continued.

"Happy b-day Bobbi. Do I need to come by myself?"

"No, if you got a friend it's okay to bring him. It's more entertainment for us," Tammy said. She had red hair and freckles with big titties and no ass, but she was bad too. London was a real red bone, very petite and quiet.

"Well I'ma bring my homeboy with me. You ladies will like him too," I told them.

"We'll see you later then," they said, and walked away. I walked in the house to see my Babygirl looking like a real queen.

"Come give your daddy some loving my little queen," I told her, wrapping her in a hug.

"Where is Sunni Daddy?" she asked.

"She's at her house. Do you want to go see her later?"

"Yes!" she said, jumping up and down.

"Well, go get you some clothes then," I told her. "Where's Kay?" I asked as Babygirl ran off down the hall.

"Looking at the TV," she shouted back.

I headed toward the living room. "What's up Kay?" I asked.

"You hear what happened to Lil Jon?" she asked.

"He killed somebody and I told the nigga to give up the dope game and get this money the right way with me," I said. "He had his chance and fucked up."

"Boy, you said that to him?" she asked.

"Not yet, but I'm planning on it. Figuring out with his business associate when I can drop in and see him. Can't you see I'm trying to keep from going back to prison?" I told her.

Kay's eyes narrowed. "Would this business associate you're talking about be a woman named D?"

"Yeah," I said, sitting down next to my sister. "Why, wassup?"

Kay shifted restlessly. "Just watch out for her. I've met her in the past and there's something about her I don't trust."

"Really? Because she runs a tight ship, I was thinking about bringing her into our business."

"Just be careful E," Kay warned. "You don't think it's a lil convenient that Lil Jon's business partner is exactly your type of woman?"

"Man I got myself a woman! I'm not looking for any others."

Kay rolled her eyes. "Yeah okay. All men are the same. All I'm saying is, be careful. Go ahead and work with this Ms. D but keep an eye on her. Lil Jon got himself into some real bad shit while you were away."

"Aight," I promised.

"So what you gonna do now?"

"Keep working on my club."

"You gotta have club money."

"I know, and I got a gig tonight stripping for this girl's birthday, me and my guy Gee," I said.

"Gee? What does he look like?" she asked. "He gonna be able to keep up with you?"

"You'll see him in a few. I gotta call him and let him know I made it."

I went to my room and texted Gee the info on how to get to my sister's, then went to see if Babygirl was ready to go.

"Babygirl, you ready?" I asked, tapping on her door.

"Yeah!" she yelled in excitement. I couldn't help but smile I called Sunni and told her to come to Kay's, that I needed her to watch Babygirl, and told her I had to do a show tonight. She told me she was on her way and would be there in an hour. After the call, I told Kay to be looking for Gee and that Sunni was on her way too.

I was in need of a shower before the night kicked off. It was 7:30 PM when I looked at my phone.

"Damn, where the time go?" I said to myself as I let the hot water rinse the grime and prison dirt off me. I showered and felt refreshed after, more refreshed than I'd felt in a while.

I threw on some of my Jordan aftershave, and lined up my goatee. I dressed in some 501 Levi's, a Polo shirt that showed off my arms and chest. Then I emerged from the bathroom and packed a work bag, which we were going to use to get ready before we arrived.

I had on some tight Ralph Lauren boxer briefs to show off my junk and thought about my Levi's and Polo boots and changed into my Jordan sweat suit, and my red black and white Jordan's. White and black Jordan shirt with the red jump man on the front. I needed something that was easy to strip out of.

I grabbed my bag and headed back to the living room, where I heard laughter, and when I rounded the corner Sunni was tickling Babygirl on the couch and Kay was helping.

"Dang, you made it here faster than an hour," I said.

"I was at the mall on University bae," she told me.

Then the doorbell rang. I headed to answer it, leaving the girls to their games. When I opened the door my guy Gee was wearing an R-neck t-shirt, jeans, and Jordan's too.

"What's good my guy? Come on in," I told him, and he followed me to the living room. "We need to get some ski masks and fake pistols bro; the cop theme is played out. We going as robbers this trip."

He just nodded and said, "Cool, cool."

When we entered the living room my sister stopped what

she was doing and stared at Gee. "Damn! Who's that?"

Gee was over saying hello to Sunni.

"Big sis, this is Gee. Gee, this is my sister Kay," I said, doing the introductions.

"How you doing?" Gee said, reaching out to shake Kay's hand.

"Close your mouth Kay," I said laughing.

"Shut up boy! Damn, I'd spend my money on you right now!" She started rubbing Gee's arms and chest.

"Well, get you and ya friends together and you can see him perform," I told her.

"I'll give them a call. Where ya'll going to be at?"

"I met these females in front of the house and today is Bobbi's b-day, and I'ma do a lil something for her," I told her. "Do you know any of them?"

"Yeah, I play cards with her and some of her friends on the weekend," she said.

"Babygirl, when I get done, I'll be joining you and Sunni tonight. Come give me a hug before you leave," I told my daughter. "And thank you bae. Do you need some money?" I asked Sunni.

"No, we good. Just hurry home and you know what I want!" she said and gave me a wink with a wicked smile.

"I got you bae," I replied, kissing her goodbye.

"See you later bae and get home safely," she said with concern.

"You ready to ride Gee? We still gotta go get that shit," I told him, waiting for him to break his conversation with Kay.

"Yeah, I'm ready, let's ride," he said, just as excited as I was to be getting this little gig.

We rode in his car because mine was blocked in. We jumped in and headed to Walmart to get some masks and black hoodies. I texted Stacey and let her know we were on our way. It was only 8:20 PM, so we might be early, but I figured it wouldn't hurt.

Twenty minutes later we pulled in at Walmart and knew what we was looking for, so we ran in and out in ten minutes. We dressed down in the car and waited to put our masks on.

"The first dollar we get tonight is getting framed," I told Gee.

"Why?"

"I'll explain it to you one day," I told him.

Before we left Walmart, a clerk eyed us, but I assured her we were male strippers and I'd give her a little preview if she wanted. The chocolate female who introduced herself as Nakita and was thick as hell said she wanted a private show and she'd text me when she got off to let me know when.

In the car my phone vibrated in my pocket. I pulled it out to see Ms. D's number on my caller ID.

"What's up boo thang?" I asked her.

"My homegirls want to kick it off tonight," she said.

"I'm busy tonight but do this for me — post the business on Facebook, and just a business number. Download that app so you don't have to use ya real number."

"What do ya boo get?"

"Just handle that business for me and I got you. I'll get at you tomorrow, I've reached my destination ma," I tell her. Before we get out the car, I ask Gee, "Man, you need something to get you going?"

"Yeah, I need a drink," he said. I told him it was a liquor store up the street, to head up there before they noticed the car. He backed up and we pulled up a few minutes later. I got out and went in and my old friend AB from Mississippi was working the counter.

"What's up E?" he asked.

"Well old school just got out the pen," I told him.

We made small talk and he was telling me about being between jobs and taking care of two kids. I told him about my stripper gig and gave him my number and told him to get at me. I got a bottle of E&J and a couple tall boys and headed back to the car.

We went back to Kay's for a second to get ourselves together as an act. We were already dressed, and they lived the way up from Kay, who wasn't home. We went over the set a couple times. Gee pulled out some of that gas and rolled him a blunt.

"Can I fire dis up?" he asked.

"Where'd you get that from?"

"I been smoking, why you want to hit this?" he asked. I hit it once because I needed my mind to stay on the bigger picture.

Stacey had already texted me and told me they in the big green house where they came walking from earlier.

"Gee, we straight now. Let me hit that one more time," I told Gee. He passed me the blunt and I hit it long and hard before I gave it back to Gee. He put it out.

"So tell me this," he said as he got himself ready in the front seat. "I know you and Sunni always had a thing…but she really okay with all this? You going out and dancing for other women, staying out all night?"

I shrugged. "I've been straight with her from the start. She knows I'm all about her. These other women are just cash rolls to me."

"All I'm saying is, if I was with a woman right now, she would not be cool with me doing this job. Only reason my baby mama isn't riding me about this is because I'm going to be bringing home that cash. There's too much temptation out there man."

I just shook my head.

"Man, on anotha note," I continued, "why you didn't look out for a nigga down there?"

"Man, I got a family to provide for. I didn't wanna lose my job," he explained.

"Okay, I feel you on that. But let's go get this money."

I put my mask on and tucked the gun on my waist, locking up my Kay's house upon leaving. We jumped in Gee's ride and went up the street to Bobbi's.

"Bruh, we gonna be harder than Chippendale's dancers," I told Gee.

We killed the car; I took a swallow of that E&J one more time and passed it to Gee before getting out. I pulled my mask down and pulled out the all black desert eagle pistol and Gee followed suit. We got to the door and the fun began.

3

WE RANG THE DOORBELL AND I waited. I could hear voices and music playing in the house. Locks began getting turned on the door and the door came open. I raised my gun to the red bone London's face, who was standing at the door wearing some booty shorts that were black and said Pink across the pussy which sat fat in them.

She had on a matching muscle shirt that showed her titties and you could see the erect nipples through the white material. Gee pushed past her and from the cars in the yard, and the voices coming from inside, they had invited a few more friends over.

I put my finger to my mouth, telling her to shush and told her if she listened, she wouldn't get hurt. She just nodded.

I pushed her back into the house, closed and locked the door. The stereo was jamming when we walked in. You could smell food, alcohol, and weed. Me and my guy were bout to turn this shit inside out.

I told London to direct us to the living room where everybody was at. She pointed, shaking badly with her wine cooler in hand. We entered the living room and there were shocked looks on some of the women's faces. All the laughing stopped, only the music played.

"Go turn that shit down!" I told London and gave her a push. When the music went down, we could hear each other.

"Everybody sit the fuck down!" Gee yelled. I could tell he was turned up. They invited two more females over and they were bad too. The thicker ones in the house and they were some chocolate twins named Tia and Toni, and they were bad. They had matching hearts with — tatted across their chests but one had a flower on her stomach and that was Tia. Toni was slightly taller. I remembered them from back before I went to the pen years ago.

"Who's the lady of the house?" I asked, pulling a chair out.

"I am," Bobbi said. "But what's going on? Just please get what you came for and leave!" She started crying.

London went and sat between Stacey and Tammy.

"Get your ass up here and shut the fuck up. Gee, cut that radio up!" I told Gee. Bobbi sat in the chair scared and confused.

I removed my hoodie to show off my cannon-like arms and removed my t-shirt, but kept my muscle shirt and mask on. Still holding my gun. Gee had his gun pointed at the women on the couch.

I removed another chair and pointed at Stacey, the lil mixed chick. She began to cry but did as she was told and sat down.

"Where the money at?" I asked over the music.

"All I got is a few thousand dollars in my purse," she said, and motioned to the pink Chanel bag on the table. I grabbed it and handed it to her.

"Stop that crying we not gonna hurt ya'll. Just be cool, and ya'll can go back to having fun," Gee said, pulling off his hoodie and v-neck. He also had on a muscle shirt.

"Ma, someone put a hit on you and the ladies were in the wrong place at the wrong time," I told Bobbi, but I was standing beside Stacey. Gee stood by Bobbi. I handed Bobbi and Stacey the paper and they looked confused. "Who going first?" I asked. They both dropped their heads.

"Leave them alone, you came for me!" Bobbi said.

"You right," Gee said. And Usher's "Nice and Slow" made perfect timing on the radio. Gee ripped off his shirt and got to gyrating and flexing in front of Bobbi, and I followed suit.

The girls got to laughing. We threw off our masks and I did a pelvic thrust, putting my dick all in Stacey's face.

Gee came out his sweats and had on a tuxedo thong. I ripped my sweats off and showed off my semi hard dick in my Ralph Lauren briefs.

They jumped up, yelling "Take them off!" But this was business. I couldn't get naked as much as I wanted. They got to stuffing money in our waistbands, and Stacey eyed that monster in her face then rubbed her face against me.

I was glad to see the ladies loosen up and start to have fun. By this time Kay and a few of her friends popped in. They went straight for their pocketbooks.

Gee seen Kay and started dancing and grinding on her too. I was kinda mad, but she was having fun and we needed to get this money, so I backed down.

We'd been dancing for a little over 2 ½ hours now. We gave the birthday girl a double-team dance before we shut it down.

We did good for the night, bringing in well over two grand a piece. That was good for the first night and it was about ten or eleven women around.

We put our sweats and shirts back on, talked for a minute before heading out. In the car Gee fired up the rest of his blunt. He passed it to me, I hit it a few times and passed it back. He cranked up the car and we headed back to Kay's so I could get my ride. I called Sunni and told bae I was on my way to her. She was sleeping, I could tell from the sound of her voice.

We made it to Kay's in a few minutes. I chucked up the deuces to Gee and he pulled off. I jumped in my BMW, pulled out and gunned it to Sunni's house.

An hour later, I was pulling up behind bae's Q50. No lights were on. I texted her and told her to let me in. When I grabbed my stuff and headed for the house she was waiting at the door in a long t-shirt and thong, hair thrown to the side. She looked so damn sexy. She gave me a long kiss before letting me in.

"How'd the night go?" she asked.

"Cool, very tiring but we made good bank. Over two grand a piece," I said.

"You hungry?" she asked.

"Yeah, and I need a shower," I told her, heading to her room. I went and cut the TV on for a minute. This infomercial was on talking about business owners. Like he was talking about me. I got into it while baby put me together something to eat. She came back with a coke, sandwich, and some chips.

"So what'd you get at the mall today?" I asked as she sat down next to me.

Sunni glanced at me. "Oh, nothing. I ended up running into an old friend and we just grabbed a bite to eat."

I ate and watched this show and went and jumped into the shower. Sunni was half asleep waiting on me when I got out, freshly cleaned and wearing a fresh pair of boxers. I climbed in and cuddled up to her, instantly dropping into a deep sleep.

—·—

I was woken up by Babygirl jumping on the bed, asking me to get up.

"I will in a few Babygirl, where's Sunni at?" I asked.

"In the kitchen cooking," she said.

"Do you like Sunni?" I asked Babygirl, pulling her into a hug and tickling her.

"Yeah, I like her, but can I finish watching TV daddy?" she asked.

I kissed her on the forehead and let her go. I jumped up and hit the shower real quick, then hit my grill before putting on a pair of gym shorts and a t-shirt and heading to the kitchen where Sunni was at the stove cooking something that smelled good.

I stood in the doorway for a second. She was wearing some gray sweats, showing off that shapely ass she got. And she was talking to someone on her phone with her back to me.

"I can't right now," I heard her say quietly. "He'll be up soon. We can talk about it later, I'll give you a call when I'm free."

She hung up the phone and leaned over the stove again. I walked up behind her and wrapped her up tight. She jumped a little but settled down when she realized it was me.

I kissed her on the neck, and she moaned a little. "I hope you hungry bae," she said.

"Yeah, I woke up starving," I told her. From the looks of it, she was making a ham and cheese omelet with onions, peppers, and bell peppers in it, and sausage in another skillet. I grabbed a seat and yelled for Babygirl to come eat as she slid my plate in front of me. She made Babygirl a small plate with juice too.

"So who was that you was talking to a few minutes ago?" I asked as I dug in.

Sunni turned back to the stove. "Hmm?" I pressed.

She turned back to me with a wide smile. "Oh, that was just my friend I was telling you I ran into yesterday. She wants to meet up tomorrow. But I told her we got a lot going on in this house — I got a man who needs his rest, after all."

She came around behind me and laid some kisses all up my neck. I pulled her into my lap and fed her some of my omelet.

By the time I finished, which was about ten minutes later, Babygirl joined us.

"You want to go to the zoo today Babygirl?" I asked. The reply I got was a squeal of 9-year-old excitement.

"I'm gonna get me another shower then," Sunni said.

"And I'm gonna get some clothes out and ready. Babygirl when you're done, let's get you a shower too and Sunni will put your hair in some pigtails for me," I said.

"Thank you daddy!" she yelled as I followed Sunni to the bedroom.

When we entered the room, Sunni pushed the door closed and pushed me against it. She dropped to her knees and gave me a sloppy blowjob, but it was good. I ran my fingers through her waist-length hair, pulled her to her feet by her hair, bent her over the bed and slammed my dick into her guts.

She bit back a moan to keep Babygirl from hearing. I felt like I was fixing to cum and then Babygirl called out for Sunni. I stroked her one more time and let her get up. She pulled her sweats up and kissed me before walking out the room.

I went to the shower to cool down before I got dressed. When I came out Sunni was getting her clothes ready for a shower. We passed each other and she gave my dick a quick squeeze before going in the bathroom and closing the door.

I went to my bag and pulled out a pair of my faded to black 501 Levi's and a plain white tee and my all white Airmax's. I got dressed real quick and sprayed on some Polo Red Cologne before going to the living room with Babygirl.

She was wearing a pink polo shirt, khaki shorts, and pink and white Nike shoes. I unplugged my phone and sat down to call and check on my business investor Ms. D. She answered after the second ring.

"Good morning handsome," she said.

"Good morning to you too."

"I need to see you before the day's out, and I need you to go pick up the business cards too," she said.

"Okay. Have you talked to my brotha yet?" I asked. She said she'd talk to me when I came over. I told her aight and hung up.

Then I called Gee real quick to let him know what's up. He answered, still sounding sleepy.

"Damn nigga you up early!" he said.

"Yeah, this money never sleeps. But I need you to meet me at Kay's around 4 so I can introduce you to my homegirl and investor," I told him.

"Alright, I got you bro," he said.

"She's gonna hook shit up for us bro and help us get to where we need to be."

"Cool. I'll meet you at 4," he said and hung up.

When I looked up, Sunni was standing there looking good and smelling good.

"What's that you wearing? It smells good," I told her.

"That's some feminine body spray," she told me. She had on a pair of Baby Phat jeans and heeled boots to match with a Baby Phat collared shirt with gold earrings. Bae looked good.

"Everybody looks ready to go to me," I said, and Babygirl finally looked up from the TV and cut it off. We headed out and Sunni wanted me to drive, so I locked up and we jumped in my red BMW and headed back to the town to hit up the zoo.

An hour later we pulled up and it was jam packed. We found a parking spot and finally got out, ready to go enjoy ourselves. As Babygirl looked at the animals, Sunni and I talked.

"So, where's her mom, if you don't mind me asking?" she said.

"Her mother Myka passed when she was just a baby," I told her. She hooked her arm through mine as Babygirl jumped an squealed looking at the lion cubs and baby elephants. We walked around for a few hours and I got Babygirl to finally eat, but when we started back up she looked tired, so I announced that it was time to go because I had some things to do.

We headed to the car and got ready to head back to Kay's spot. I looked in the rearview mirror at my daughter starting to doze off and told Sunni, "I'ma give her the world."

We drove in silence, letting my Babygirl sleep. We finally made it to Kay's and I pulled in behind Sunni's parked car. I got out and carefully picked up Babygirl to carry her in the house.

When we entered the house Kay was drinking, so I went to lay my daughter down, and after I got her situated I went to join bae and my sister in the living room where Sunni had made herself a drink.

"Girl! You should've been there last night," Kay was telling her.

"I know right!" she replied, cocking an eyebrow at me.

"She gonna get a private show later on," I told them and I noticed Sunni's cheeks get red.

"So how much bread did ya'll make last night, bro?" Kay asked me. I leaned back in the loveseat and pondered on what we made.

"A little over two bands," I said.

"Damn! I think I need to start stripping, huh?" Kay said.

"Me too," Sunni chimed in. I just laughed. I looked at

my phone to check the time and saw it was 3:50PM. A few minutes later there was a knock on the door, and I knew it was Gee.

I kissed Sunni goodbye and Kay too and told bae I'd be with her later. I stepped outside and shook hands with Gee. I looked at my watch and it was 4PM. Gee and I jumped in his ride and headed to meet Ms. D.

We got to Ms. D's house and she must have heard the car because she met us at the door.

"I wish you came this morning to break me off some of that," she said, and came up on her tiptoes to kiss me.

"Maybe next time," I told her.

Kim came from the back as Gee was stepping in the house and closing the door.

"Gee this thick blonde with the glasses is Ms. D. That's her friend, Kim," I said, doin the introductions. Gee looked at Ms. D and his eyes stayed glued to that ass. We gave him the rundown about our business on Facebook.

"We need you to holla at some of them dudes at your job, because we got work to a year and we need the extra help," I told Gee.

"I'ma get at em and see what's shaking, and if they with it, I'ma tell em to let the other job go," Gee said.

"Shit bro, we gonna get this real money. It's all coming in one night," I told him.

"Look daddy! We got some hits now and the page ain't been jumping long!" Kim said from her laptop on the kitchen counter. We went to take a look, and then Tana comes from the back on her tablet.

"See bro, we got females from all over that want to book shows," I told him.

"Ya'll got one Monday night too. Some woman named

Donna just in boxed me saying her friend's having a party and ya'll need to be there by 9:30," Ms. D said.

"We got her," Gee said. I told Gee we needed to hit the gym tomorrow night before we go to Ms. Donna's for the gig. I had Ms. D look AB up and have him call me before Monday night. She asked me about the cards, and I handed them to her.

"The cost was $50 for a bundle of 1,000," I said. She gave me $50 plus an extra $25.

"Thank you," she said. "The phone's been ringing off the hook and I know you, Tana and Kim have been working ya'lls ass off for this business," I said. "We don't have to fuck wit no drugs," I added, and everyone agreed. "Also, we are going to have a sit down to talk about this business taking off like a rocket and everyone on the team needs to be here. But we gotta be out. Ya'll take care and keep me updated," I said, kissing Ms. D on the forehead before we left.

We got back to the car and before we pulled off Gee rolled and fired up another blunt. I asked to hit it and took a few pulls on it before I passed it back.

"Man, go on an stop by the liquor store before you drop me off. I'm feeling good and about bout to go fuck the shit outta my girl," I tell him.

"I got you boss man," he replied.

Some minutes later we pulled up to the liquor store and I got out and run in real quick. I got me a couple of tall cans when somebody starts calling my name. I look around to see my ex girl Young standing there.

"What's been up with you Big E?" she asked.

"Just got out and working on my business," I told her, leaning up against the counter.

"How's Kay doing?"

"She's alright, her and Babygirl, who's 9 now. So how's ya fam doing?"

"Well the family is Gucci and I'm married now with two kids. They're getting bigga every day."

"That's what's up, and you still look good too," I told her.

"Thank you."

I handed her one of my business cards and waited as she read it.

"Male strippers?" she asked with a shocked look on her face.

"Yup, that's what I do now," I replied.

"Finally, we got something like that down here," she said.

"Well I gotta get going. Give me a call if you ever want some entertainment or want to have fun," I said, and gave her a hug before leaving. I got back in the car and we headed back to Kay's house.

"Man, who was that, because you got hoes everywhere," Gee said.

"Just my ex, and she say she married now," I tell him.

"Cool," he said as we pulled into Kay's driveway.

"I'll see you tomorrow bro, and gym call at 12 noon. Gotta get it early," I said and closed the door. The first thing I did when I got in the house was go check on my daughter. Then I checked on Kay, who was passed out in the den. I went to the living room and cut the TV on MTV Cribs re-runs. As I was drinking on my old E tall boy my phone gets to ringing. It was a number I didn't know.

"Hello, who dis?" I asked, rolling a blunt Gee gave me.

"This T-baby. Is Big E around?" she asked.

"This is he. What's up ma?"

"Didn't think you'd hear from me huh?" she asked.

"You must've gotten my number from my bro before he got fucked up?"

"Yeah, hope that was okay. So what's up?"

"Nothing, just getting myself back to the world after being gone ten years," I said. I fire up the blunt. "What about you?" I asked.

"Not shit, working."

"Can a brotha take a beautiful sista to eat?" I asked.

"Sure, when's good for you?"

"Thursday, how's that sound?"

"Cool with me," she said.

"Cool, because I'd like to get to know you as well," I told her.

"Okay, key my number in and I'll see you Thursday."

"Take care of yourself," I said and hung up to enjoy my blunt and beer.

I gave my friend Joey a call, but no one answered so I figured I'd try back later. I gather myself and get ready to head back to Sunni's tonight. I went and gave Babygirl a kiss and love before checking on Kay, who was still out of it.

I put $150 by the TV and cut it off before getting my beer and half smoked blunt and heading out.

Getting in the car, I started toward Dumas. I fired down on the rest of my blunt and pulled out my phone to call bae.

"Hey   Daddy,   what   you   doing?"
"Drinking a little. Getting myself together for you," I said.

"Where you at?"

"I'm on my way, so be naked when I get there because it's going down," I tell her. I finished off my blunt and beer, buzzed and high as hell. By the time I pull up to Sunni's I was feeling good about myself.

I parked and headed in the house, kicking off my clothes as I made my way toward the bedroom. Reaching the door, I got a view of Sunni laid out on the bed, knees up, spread eagle, digging in the pussy. My dick jumped to life instantly.

"This what you want daddy?" she asked, spreading that pretty peach colored pussy, giving me a good look.

"Hell yeah!" I said excitedly.

I entered the room and crawled up the bed and kissed up the insides of her long ass legs and smooth thighs. Then I hit her center and inhaled the sweet smell coming off her pussy. I start placing kisses on her clit, spreading her lips with my tongue, licking from her pussy hole back to her clit and giving it a long hard suck.

She came immediately.

I flipped her over and raised her ass up, face down. She reached under her and rubbed her clit, moaning softly.

"Mmmm...give it to me just how you want to daddy!" I placed kisses all over her round, sexy ass. Spreading them thick cheeks, I licked around her asshole, and slowly penetrated it with my tongue, and she threw that ass back, letting me know she wanted more. By this time I was hard as a rock.

She began to shake and I knew she was cumming again. "Give me that dick baby!" she growled.

I raised up and placed my dick at her pussy hole. I rubbed it up and down the folds of her pussy and when I was at her entrance she threw it back on me again, sliding that dick all the way in her guts.

She gasped for air. I slowly dug into the pussy, moving in and out real slow. She began twerking on my dick so I started pounding her walls until I feel this warm liquid roll down my leg. She squirted all over me and the bed. I pulled out and placed that dick at the entrance of her asshole next.

"Baby! You're too big, it won't fit!" she said, but she began pushing back on it. Slowly she opened up to me, drawing a groan from deep inside my throat.

After a couple minutes, I was all the way in her ass to the hilt and gave her a minute to adjust. She flexed her muscles around me before I got to pumping in her in long, steady strokes. I knew I wasn't going to last long because her shit was tight.

"Fuck my ass daddy and cum in it!" she begged.

I began pounding her with long, hard, slow strokes. I busted all in her ass after a few minutes. Let my dick go soft before pulling out. I fell beside her on the bed.

"Nigga we ain't done!" she said and went to the bathroom. I could hear water running.

She comes out with a wet rag and wipes off my soft dick and instantly it's coming back to life with just the touch of her soft hands. She placed kisses and licks over it and swallowed it slow.

I looked at the bedside clock and it's 10:39PM. She climbed on top and fucked me like it was going outta style. We finally passed out at around 2:45AM. Sunni fell asleep on top of me. She woke up to her phone vibrating and it was Babygirl.

"Baby, Babygirl on the phone," she said, shaking me fully awake. I looked over at the clock and it was 7:30AM. I jumped up.

"Damn, I gotta go. I got some shit to handle."

I looked at my phone and had some missed calls from Ms. D. I jumped in the shower real quick, jumped out and dressed down in a Polo shirt, Levi's and J's.

"You want something to eat before you leave?" Sunni asked.

"Nah, I'm straight. I'ma pick something up on the way," I told her. "But can you go get Babygirl for me?"

"Yeah, I got you bae," she said. I kissed bae on the forehead and headed out the door.

As I left, I texted Sunni and told her to meet me at Kay's around 6 or so. I jumped in my BMW and as I'm pulling out and leaving I called Gee.

"Be at Kay's around 6 or so," I told him. "And make sure you meet me at the gym Monday too, so we can see what we got," I added.

Pulling up at Ms. D's spot, I hurried to park. Before I could knock on the door, she had already snatched it open. She snatched me into a kiss.

It caught me off guard but I walked her to the bedroom, never breaking contact. I played with that fat ass of hers while we stripped each other's clothes off. Once naked, I bent her over the side of the bed.

"Go on tear this shit up. You know you've been wanting to," she said, making that ass clap. I rammed that dick in her from the back and pounded away at her tight walls, with her screaming and moaning.

"Ohhh! Fuck me daddy. Break this pussy in half," she panted.

I gripped them hips tighter and pounded them guts as hard and far as I could go. She came hard and I pulled out and she must've read my mind, because she reached back and spread that ass for me.

I know white girls are freaks, but damn, I thought.

I slowly pushed into her asshole and she opened right up, letting me know she's with the anal play. I got to thinking about Sunni, got my dick in Ms. D's ass, and I pulled out and headed to the shower.

She came in behind me and asked, "What's up with you!?"

"Got some shit on my mind, and I'm trying to keep it professional between us," I said.

She stepped her thick ass in the shower and wrapped her arms around me, laying her head on my back.

"Just give me a fix and I won't ask anymore," she said.

I bent her over on the back shower wall, she leaned on

the wall and stuck that thick shapely ass out, and I was hard instantly. I stroked myself a couple of times and slid back in that pussy from behind, and gave her exactly what she wanted, digging off in that pussy until she was begging me to stop.

I came long and hard and rested my head on her shoulder. I washed up and rinsed off quickly and let her have the shower.

When I got dressed and go to the back room, I got smirks from Tana and Kim.

"Don't say shit," I tell em, trying not to smile.

"Why you say that? We heard her screaming ya name," Kim said. That made me feel good, because I put it down, I thought to myself. Ms. D came in a little while later and she got the same smile, she was walking stiff.

"Look what you've done!"

"It was good though."

"Sho was, I'm not complaining!" she said with a smart mouth.

"What's good on the business tip though?" I asked.

"Same old. Women everywhere trying to see ya'll," Tana said.

"Okay. Book em. Me and Gee can do a show and whoever else joins the team can do other shows," I replied. "I'm get with everyone joining. We 'pose to meet at Kay's later. Did you get at AB?" I asked.

"No," Kim said.

"Find him and let him know to get at me ASAP," I told her. She found him on Facebook and gave me his number. About thirty minutes later I called it.

"Yeah, who dis?" AB answered.

"This Big E. What's up with it?"

"I was just gonna call when I got myself right," AB said.

"Do you remember where Kay lives?"

"Yeah."

"Well be there by six," I tell him. I had some plans in my head that I wanted to run by Sunni later.

"Ms. D, here's $350 to put on Lil Jon's books. Tell him I send my love and I'll be up there to see him when I'm not busy," I told her, handing her the bills. "Well I'm out and I'll see ya'll later."

"Okay," the ladies replied together.

"Don't forget Kay's at 6."

I headed out and jumped in my ride, pulling my phone out and texting Sunni to ask where she's at.

The store, she shot back fast.

I made it to Dumas about an hour later. I got to the house and didn't see Sunni's car, so I went in and got comfortable watching TV. It was only 1:30PM. A while later Babygirl and Sunni came walking in.

"What ya'll do all morning?"

"Had girl time," Sunni answered.

"You have fun?" I ask Babygirl.

"Yes," she replied. "Sunni taking me to her mama's house tonight, she coming to get us later."

"Why didn't you tell me?" I asked, looking to Sunni. "You got some shit to do and can't watch her yourself?

"Because she wants to go, E," she said. "And I told you, I got a friend to meet up with."

Our conversation ended when the doorbell rang. I go to answer, and it was Sunni's mom. She was a spitting image of her mom.

"How're you doing Big E?" she asked.

"I'm good Mama G, thank you," I replied. I gave Babygirl $20 and a hug and told her to mind her manners.

I locked the door behind them when they left and went to the bedroom, then called to Sunni to come to me. When she did, I stripped her naked and made love to her for hours.

It was 4PM when we came up for air. I jumped in the shower and she wasn't too far behind.

After about 15 minutes I got out and dried off. When Sunni came into the room I was already dressed.

"Bae, what you think about a male stripper magazine? Or hard body magazine?"

"Sounds good, put it to work bae," she said. "See, you got ideas. You don't need to sell dope," she said.

"I'm not bae, and I want you to know that I love you."

"Love you too," she replied. "I just want you to be careful. I know you're working with your bro's business partners, and those people don't always get out the game when they should. Even if it looks like they did."

"I don't know if Ms. D and her girls could handle the dope game by themselves," I told her.

Sunni just shook her head. "He might not be in the house with them, but that doesn't mean he ain't giving them advice from behind those prison walls. Your bro wasn't running that shit all by himself E. All I'm saying is, be careful."

"I will mama," I said, leaning over to kiss her.

We were dressed and heading out the house going back to town. "E, have you been smoking weed in here," she asked, getting in my car.

I nodded.

"Well don't. Your business going first before you start kicking it," she said. "Don't tell the others yet. See how this goes first," she said as we pulled off. We made it to Kay's and were greeted by her upon entering the house.

"Hey ya'll! What's going on?" Kay asked.

"Nothing much, getting ready to handle this business. Kay, just sit back and watch brother work."

4

I LOOKED AT THE TIME. It was 5:45PM.

"They should be starting to arrive now," I said to myself, and just then the doorbell rang. I went to get it and when I opened the door it was like they all arrived together. There was Ms. D and her crew, and Gee, and some of the guys from the prison he worked at. I gave the ladies hugs and the guys dap.

"Man, what's been up with ya'll?" I asked.

"Shit, working for the state, that's it," one of the guys says. I showed everyone to Kay's den, where there were more seats, and Kay had prepared a little finger food and drinks.

"Like I told Gee, when ya'll see this money, ya'll gonna let that go," I said. The doorbell rang again, and I went to check to see who it was and finally AB was at the door. "Come on in and follow me, we just getting started," I tell him.

He followed me to the den and took a seat beside the fellas.

"I hope everyone comfortable, but we're already familiar with each other," I began once everyone quieted down. "As you know I'm CEO, and Gee is my business partner. My girl Sunni is over the accounting and Kay, my sister, is going to be our travel agent. I'm trying to take this statewide and from state to state. Ms. D, Kim, and Tana are booking the shows for us. We just gotta thank these women for their hard work."

The men all nodded their thanks to the women, and I continued on. "But to introduce the other fellas — this here AB, AKA Candyman. Then we have Sam AKA Young Payday. Behind him is Stephon and we call him Mr. Cool Off. And last but not least we have Raheem, AKA Young Hard Body. Ya'll are the stars. It's six of us for now, but as the business grows, the numbers will grow. Ya'll will get paid good, so don't get discouraged."

I then added, "If you want to lay off your other job go ahead, we not forcing you though. We working toward getting this club up and running. Everybody gonna eat alright," I said and they nodded. "I got something else in the works, haven't talked to Gee yet but Sunni likes it so be on stand by for that."

By this time Ms. D eye balling a nigga and I was hoping Sunni didn't notice that shit.

I called Gee to the kitchen, and I told him, "Man, I fucked up for real!"

"Whatchu do?" he ask.

"I put that dick in Ms. D and I don't want her to fuck shit up with Sunni," I replied.

"You know you don't mix business with pleasure. You know she gonna wanna fuck again," he said, shaking his head.

"I know. But we have other concerns now. I've come up with an idea to start a magazine as well with the same name as our business. 'Hard Body Strippers.' I'ma get some folks about this too. I'ma have it set up for female prisoners, too."

"Man, I like that idea," Gee replied.

"Don't tell them about it yet," I told Gee.

We went back to the living room. The guys were practicing dances for the women and these dudes had the moves. I had no doubt we were gonna get that paper. They were having a good time, but Ms. D was mugging me again and I looked at Gee, who followed my eyes. He seen the stare and got up to go freak on Ms. D and she enjoyed the attention.

Sunni came and sat beside me. I kissed her and told her I loved her. She replied with the same. "I love you too."

"Ya'll enjoy, and guys Monday at noon, Gee will text ya'll about what gym to meet us at. But I gotta go. See ya'll later," I said, and me and bae headed back home to her place. We got in the car and pulled off.

"Why was Ms. D looking atcha like that?" Sunni asked.

"I don't know. She had a stick up her ass today," I said. I thought to myself, *Never again.* I knew I had fucked up and knew it was a matter of time before she got me fucked off, or at least tried.

We finally make it back to Sunni's house. I got out and went to unlock the house for us. When we got inside, and I went straight to the living room to kick off my shoes and relax for a minute before taking me a shower.

"Bae, what do you plan on cooking tonight?"

"I don't know, what do you want?" she asked.

"Can you make some beef stew and mashed potatoes if that's not asking too much?"

"Yeah, I got you love," she replied. I kissed Sunni on her cheek and headed to take a quick shower.

About 30 minutes later I emerged from the bathroom with the house smelling good. I get to my drawer with a towel around me and grab a t-shirt and a pair of Joe Boxers.

I wished I had a blunt but thought about what Sunni said. I went back to the living room and watched ESPN until she was done cooking.

I went and made me a quick drink of brandy on the rocks to help me relax. I called my nigga Gee and told him to drop me off some of that gas. I hit the alarm switch on my keys so he could put it in my car like I asked.

He said him and some of the fellas was still at Kay's, but Ms. D went home, and that he'd text me when he was done there. A nigga felt a little geeked up tonight, so Sunni could get it on her mind later on.

Bae came in and took the glass outta my hand.

"We can drink later," she said with a wink before her phone started to ring. We figured it was Babygirl calling from her mom's, and it was.

"Hey Babygirl, how's everything going?"

"Good, we're making cookies and stuff. Is my dad around?" Babygirl asked.

"Yeah, hold on." Sunni passed me the phone.

"Hey Babygirl," I said. "Are you enjoying yourself and being good?"

"Yes sir, we're making cookies, do you want me to bring you some? Karis and Shalondon made some too, but Daddy I want to come and stay with you and Sunni," she whined.

"We'll see how later looks."

"Okay, love you daddy. Can I talk to Sunni again?" Babygirl asked.

After bae got done talking to Babygirl, I asked her, "Who is Karis and Shalondon?"

"They're my nieces," she replied.

"Oh, okay."

Then she went to check the food, and I got the text from Gee letting me know it's done. Now I wanted to go to my car and put one in me, but I know Sunni's going to be wondering what I'm doing, so I just sit tight watching TV.

About thirty minutes later, she came in the living room carrying steaming bowls of stew and potatoes. She popped in a movie and came to sit beside me. After we get done eating,

I put our plates on the table and pulled her into my arms to cuddle to the rest of her movie, *Basic Instinct*.

"It feels good to be home," I told her, pulling her in tight and kissing her cheek. "I ain't selling dope no mo, and I can actually spend time with my daughter, and I got a good woman in my life," I added.

"Oh, your daughter asked could she come stay with us. I don't mind, you're my man, and she's become my baby girl too," Sunni said. "You were put in my life for a reason, E."

"When I get done, I'ma make sure you and Babygirl don't ever go without," I tell her. "When my lil bro picked me up, I told him I'm done selling dope, that I wanna live right this time. Look at me and him. If I left with him that night and not here with you, I'd be beside him. I gave Ms. D $350 for him. I'll go see him when the time is right," I said.

"Bae, you're a good man, just got mixed with the wrong crowd," she said. This is the same thing she used to tell me when I was in the pen and we'd get to talking. "Just be careful around your bro. You'd be surprised what niggas can accomplish even locked up. And I'm not liking the way Ms. D had her eyes on you tonight."

"There's nothing you gotta worry about bae. I made it clear when he picked me up that I ain't going back to that shit. He knows better than to try and involve me in any of his game. I already done more than enough for him by serving those ten years."

By this time, the movie was going off.

I thought, *When my money gets right, I'ma get him a good lawyer to come home.*

Lil Jon might've done me wrong by letting me take the fall for that bust all those years ago, but we had a history. Although we weren't blood related he grew up with me and Kay — raised by our grandma — and so it was hard to see him locked away. Especially hard for Kay, who had always tried to talk him out of his bad decisions.

We headed to the bedroom, cutting the living room TV off. I jumped in the bed and cut our TV on. I pulled her into the bed with me and start placing kisses all over her.

"Bae let me get a shower!" she begged.

I laughed and let her go.

While she showered, I ran to the car and fired down on a blunt Gee had already rolled for me. I hit it a few times before putting it out and heading back inside. When I moved it back to the room, I laid down, enjoying my high before she came walking out. In a lace bra and some booty shorts, hair damp. But she smelled good. She looked at me and asked, "Why your eyes red?"

"I was falling asleep bae," I told her. She cut the TV off and cuddled up to me.

———•———

Early Sunday she woke me and asked, "You want to go to church with me?"

"Nah, I got a lot to do. I've never been to church, but I promise I'll go one day," I told her.

What was on my mind was my blunt.

"Bae, you want something to eat before I leave?" she asked.

"Nah, I'll get something later. But when you get home, I'll have your dinner made," I promised. She went to finish getting dressed, and then came back and said, "You don't know how to cook," and smiled.

I went to the kitchen to take us out something to eat. After that I went back to the living room and watched some TV. She came out the room dressed in a Chanel dress and heels, looking extremely beautiful. I walked her to her car to see her off.

When she left, I went to my car and put some heat behind the rest of my blunt. After I knocked off the rest of the blunt, I went in the house and called Gee and told him to get me a QP ready, so I could have my own stash here at home.

I then needed to call Ms. D, because I felt like she was gonna get on some bullshit. She didn't answer the first time so I waited a little minute.

She called back about thirty minutes later.

"You called me?"

"Yeah, you need to chill the fuck out like for real!" I yelled.

"Fuck you!" she yelled back and hung up.

Before I could set my phone down Gee called and told me I needed $300 for my QP. I agreed and we hung up, I went to check on the chicken I had out getting ready to cook later. I threw on a t-shirt, and my Airmax 90s, grabbed my keys, and headed out to meet Gee.

After a 30-minute drive to Wrightsville, I pulled up at Gee's house. It was a green Yukon Denali parked in the front yard. I parked behind it, got out, and went to the door. After knocking a couple times Gee finally opened the door.

"What's good bro?"

"Man, I came to pick that up so I can get back home to cook for Sunni," I told him.

"Come on to the back real quick," he said, motioning me in.

We go to the back and it was another cat in the room. "This is my family Roseby, but we call him Black," Gee said.

"What's good fam, they call me Big E. Gee, is this that good shit?" I asked.

"Yeah, I got you fam," Gee said.

"And don't forget to be at the gym tomorrow afternoon," I said before turning back to Roseby. "Good looking out fam, do you got a number I can reach you when I want some more?"

He gave me a number and I gave him and Gee some dap before heading out. I got back to my car and headed out. When I made it home, I left the weed in the car so Sunni wouldn't get mad at me.

I got out that Sunday morning heat and got in the house to the cool air before going to the kitchen to start frying this chicken and putting the biscuits in the oven with gravy, rice, and green beans.

While I was cooking and listening to ESPN on the TV from the living room, my phone rang and I pulled it out and see Ms. D's number across my screen.

"What's up?"

"What's up Big E?"

"Nothing, what the fuck is up with you and why you wig out last night?" I asked.

"Because I want you to myself!" she cried.

"Ma, I've got a woman and we agreed to it only being one time," I told her. "So we need to keep this shit on a professional level."

"Okay," she said.

"Don't ever pull no stunt like that again, understood?" I tell her.

"Yes E. Before I forget, I went to see your brother and put that money on his books."

"Cool. I'll see you tomorrow, so be looking for me. And be ready to jump this business off."

I didn't give her time to reply and hung up. I was feeling Ms. D, but I knew I wouldn't be able to have my cake and eat it too. When I looked up it was turning 1PM. I had just got done cooking and sat down to watch more ESPN when I heard the locks in the door and in came Babygirl and Sunni.

"There goes my favorite women. Ya'll have a good time at church?" I asked.

"Yeah," Babygirl said.

"And where's my cookies at lil girl?" I asked, tugging on her pigtails.

"They're gone, I didn't think you were serious daddy!" she squealed, pulling away from me.

"I was forreal. You owe me a kiss to pay for my cookies," I said, and she gave me a kiss on the cheek.

"It smells good in here!" Sunni said.

"I know," I replied, tone cocky.

We got into the kitchen and washed up for lunch. We sat and talked about church, and bae said her mom asked why I didn't come with them. I told her one day I will. Sunni prayed and took the first bite.

"Mmmm...bae, this is good! You're going to be cooking for us all the time," she said.

"I told you daddy can cook!" Babygirl said. When we got done eating, I went to the bedroom to lay down for a minute. Babygirl came in a little while later and jumped in the bed with me.

"Daddy are we going to get a bigger house?" she asked.

"Yeah, and like I told you, you can have whatever you want and I'm forreal about that," I told her.

She hugged me and told me not to go away again, that she wanted me out here with her and Sunni. I hugged her tight and she went back to the living room. My lil girl touched my heart and brought tears to my eyes. Sunni came in.

"What's wrong baby?" she asked, seeing the look on my face.

"For a 9-year-old, my baby is very smart," I said. "When

school starts back up, I want Babygirl living with us and I want you to stay working at the pen and get back in school, so you can get your degree in Business & Management. You'll be able to get a business and open up the club for us."

"Okay," she said, cutting on the TV and lying beside me. I drifted off to sleep even though it was still early in the day, because I knew I had a long day ahead of me.

———•———

When I got up the next morning, I went to get us breakfast. I got some cheesy eggs, toast, and hash browns. While I was gone, I smoked me a blunt to start the day off mellow. Waffle House was up the street, so I didn't have to travel far. When I made it back to the house Babygirl was up watching TV, and I told her to wash up for breakfast.

I took Sunni her breakfast while in bed. I poured her some juice as well because she loves orange juice. I went into the room, she still in the bed. I sat her food on the nightstand and woke her up to eat.

"Bae here goes breakfast, so wake ya ass up and eat," I told her.

"Thank you," she mumbled, and rolled over and looked at me for a second before sitting up. Her phone lit up on the nightstand and as soon as I glanced at it, she snatched it up.

"Probably just my momma," she said, tucking it up next to her. I narrowed my eyes at her, but went to check on Babygirl. She was acting a little weird sometimes and I'd have to figure out why.

While she ate in peace, I went to eat with Babygirl. She was still talking about staying with us, and I told her, "We'll have to see how things go and what Kay says."

"But I'm your daughter, not hers," Babygirl said with a pout.

"Just eat and we'll talk about it later!" I told her.

I finished, got up, and went to brush my teeth and wash my face and get ready to hit the gym. In the bedroom I told Sunni, "Well bae, I'm about to hit the gym and get ready for our show tonight. I need to get the address for the guys so they can show up when they need to."

I kissed her and headed out the door. I jumped in my car and pulled out my phone to call Ms. D.

"What's up?" she answered.

"When I leave the gym, I'ma swing by there, and you can let me in on everything tonight. We can direct the guys to their parties. Oh, and what do you have on this morning?" I couldn't help myself, thinking about that thick ass.

"Why? You don't want this."

"We shall see when I get there."

"Fuck you E! Bye!" And she hung up on me. I really had this woman's nose wide open. I called Gee next; he answered on the 3rd ring.

"Where you at?" I asked him.

"On my way to the gym."

"Did you call the guys to see what's up?"

"Yeah, they gonna meet us there," Gee said.

"Okay, I'll be there soon." And we disconnected.

After a twenty minute drive, I pulled up at Planet Fitness in Little Rock. I parked beside Gee's Challenger and grabbed my bag. When I make it inside, I seen Gee and the crew stretching and getting ready.

5

WE STARTED OUR WORKOUT AROUND 9:30AM and now it was about 12:47PM. We wrapped up our session and I told them, "I will give you a call and let ya'll know where ya'll going. AB, you and Stephon gonna thug together and Sam, you and Thorne are gonna thug together. Ya'll already know it's me and Gee working together. But I'm bout to go check on this business, so ya'll be looking for my call or text."

I gave the fellas some daps and headed out to Ms. D's house to check on our shows. In the car, I fired up a blunt that I rolled this morning. I cranked up that "Run the Streetz" by Tupac and headed to the spot.

When I pulled up to Ms. D's crib, I seen her Lexus parked outside and a pearl white drop top Monte Carlo SS on 22-inch rims. I knew that was Kim's car because Tana wrecked her Maxima. I parked behind Kim and finished my blunt before going to the door. It was locked, so I rang the doorbell. Kim answered about a minute later.

"What's up E?" she asked.

"I'm good Ms. Kim, where D cry baby ass at?" I ask.

"She in her room," she replied.

I go to her room and knocked before going in. She was laying in the bed playing with her phone. She looked up.

"What're you doing?" she snapped with an attitude.

"Stop playing, you know you want this dick again." I walked over to the bed and started kissing on her, and she pushed me back and told me to stop. She didn't want to get me in trouble. I backed away and smiled and went to jump into a quick shower. By the time I got out, she was laying on her side still playing on her phone.

I dropped my towel and put my dick in her face. She just looked at me, and then I snatched the blanket off her and she was naked. I pushed her on her back and start sucking on them 34 D titties.

She dropped her phone and started moaning and grabbed my head. I then started placing kisses down her chest, licking round her navel, then reached her sweet love spot. Again, I could smell the heat rising off her. I got down on eating that pussy.

"Mmmm...just like that! You know what a bitch be wanting!" she moaned. She started shaking and I knew she was cumming, and hard, because she clutched my head with her thighs. I raised up and stroked my hard on, and she pushed up on her elbows, then came to the edge of the bed and grabbed ahold of my dick, stroking me slowly.

"Go on and handle that business, you know you wanna taste that dick!" I told her, and with that she sucked a nigga dick to kingdom come. Then I pulled it out her mouth, making a loud sucking sound.

I shoved her legs open and slammed this dick as far as it would go. For the next two hours we went at it, and finally I came on her stomach and pussy.

I rose up and went to take a quick shower. When I got out, she jumped in real quick. About 30 minutes later she came out smelling good in a beach towel. She threw on some booty shorts and a t-shirt. I threw on some shorts and a v-neck I had over here and followed her to the other room where Kim and Tana was at.

"What we got for tonight ladies?" I asked.

"Well, Donna Walker in J-ville, which you and Gee are familiar with her, so that's ya'lls show."

"Cool, where we gonna send AB and Pugh?" I asked, sitting down between the ladies.

"Kelly Jones in West Little Rock, and for Hawthorne and Walker, we got a Keisha Cathey from the Bluff. And someone wants Tuesday night too," Kim says.

"We gonna stay in the state until we stack our bread!" I said with a grin.

Then I walked into the kitchen to see what Ms. D was doing, and whatever she was throwing together smelled good.

"When can I get my own key?" I asked, leaning on the counter.

"When you stop playing games," she said.

"Why you say that?"

"Because one minute you want to fuck with a bitch, then the next you don't." She glared at me.

"Yeah, I guess you're right, it is good." I responded. With that said I told her to have me a key made, then I went to sit in the living room and scroll through the TV and do some thinking.

My phone started to ring, jarring me from my thoughts of the club and all I wanted to get done. Looking at the name on the screen, it was Sunni.

"What's up bae?"

"Where you at?" she asked.

"At Ms. D's house, why what's up?"

"When will you be home?"

"In 'bout an hour."

"Okay, luh you."

"Love you too," I replied, and disconnected the call.

About 20 minutes later Ms. D came into the living room with what she was cooking. She handed me a plate of leftover steak and a baked potato.

"Preciate it ma," I told her.

"With ya big hungry ass," she replied. Then her phone started to ring. She answered and told me it was my lil bro calling from da county. She let him know I was here and handed me the phone.

"What's good lil bro? Did you get that paper?" I asked.

"Yeah, preciate it, but I really need to see you and discuss this business," he said.

"I get you fam, but you know a nigga ain't fucking with dope," I reminded him.

"Nah bro, I need to talk to you bout my house and shit."

"Alright, I got you," I told him.

"Cool, come up here Sunday and don't tell Ms. D about anything we've discussed," he said. I passed the phone back to Ms. D.

By this time Kim came back in the room and I asked her to call up all the guys and let them know where they're needed. I gave her the names and numbers, reminded her to remind them to be on time and to find them something to perform in. "Tell them they'll get paid tomorrow, and to work with me," I told her, and she relayed the message to the group.

"Hey E!" Ms. D called as I stood, "your bro got a safe here — why don't you let me keep the cash on hand here? That way I can keep track of finances and you can let me know when you need a stack."

"I don't think so ma," I told her. "I have a set up at Sunni's for that. I'd rather keep track of how much we're bringing in myself. But I appreciate you wanting to help."

With that I got up to leave and Ms. D walked me to my car. She gave me a deep kiss and before I pulled off she dropped a key through the window into my lap and told me she loved.

As she walked off she was putting an extra twitch to them hips. She knew I had love for her, but I couldn't let it come out my mouth because I'd be fucking up then.

I pulled out a blunt from the glove compartment and fired it up. I gave Kay a call on my way back to the house. She answered after the 3rd ring.

"Damn nigga took you long enough!" I said, giving her a hard time.

"Boy hush!" she replied.

"What's good with you?"

"Not shit, watching TV bored as hell."

"Why don't you and Sunni go out sometime?" I asked her.

"I'll call her and see what's up."

"Shit, I'll have Babygirl while ya'll go out, so don't worry about that. Okay, I gotta holla atcha about her anyways."

"What she do?" Kay asked.

"Not shit, we'll talk tomorrow so be looking for me to swing by," I told her.

She blew me a kiss and hung up. By this time I finished my blunt while pulling up to the house. Two other cars were in my driveway and I'm trying to figure out who they are. I pulled up behind Sunni's car and headed toward the house. It was still early in the day and it was hot as hell already.

I got in the house and was welcomed be a cool breeze and laughter coming from the living room. I made it to the living room and Sunni and some females were watching a Tyler Perry movie and having a good time. I greeted everyone before heading to our room to get a little rest before I gotta do these shows tonight.

Sunni followed me into the room just as I was kicking my shoes off and laying back on the bed.

"What's up with you?" she asked.

"Nothing, just gotta get some sleep before these shows tonight. Why, what's up?"

"Just wanted to see if you wanted to watch this movie with me, my nieces, sista, and homegirls."

"Bae, I gotta get this business going and then I have to get my workout in, because I know you want to see your man with a nice body," I told her.

She nodded and kissed me before going back into the living room with her company. Once I closed my eyes I drifted off into an instant sleep.

When I woke up its 7:30PM. So I hopped up, grabbed me a quick shower, and got dressed. After I sprayed on some of my Polo cologne, I went to check on Babygirl, but she wasn't in her room.

I went to find Sunni. She was nowhere to be found either. So I went back to our room and put on this fake cop outfit for tonight. I called my nigga Gee when I got done putting on the uniform. He answered, "What's good E?"

"Not shit, getting ready. I'll be out that way bout 9:30, so be looking for me." We hung up. By this time Babygirl and Sunni were coming back into the house.

Babygirl looked at me and her eyes got big. "Dang daddy, you're a cop? You've been to prison!"

"Nah, but I know I look like one. But this is a long story and when you're older, I'll tell you about it," I promised her.

At the same time Sunni came in and told me I looked good and that one day I gotta arrest her for being a bad girl. She smiled that exotic smile that got me from the first time we met.

"Can I get a bite to eat before I bounce out?" I asked Sunni.

"You know you can get more than a bite to eat!" she said. I couldn't help but smile as she headed toward the kitchen.

I asked Babygirl to go grab my phone for me, so I can hit up the fellas. She came back in with it a minute later. I gave her a peck on the cheek and she sat on the couch and channel surfed the TV. I hit Sam up first and he answered on the second ring.

"What's up Big E?"

"Not too much, you and Raheem know where ya'll supposed to be at?" I asked him.

"Yeah homie, stop sweating we got this."

"Aight cool, then tomorrow ya'll meet me at Kay's house so ya'll can get paid."

"Bet that up. We'll get at you tomorrow." And he hung up.

Next I hit up Young Stephon. He told me the same thing, so I gave him the same message — be at Kay's tomorrow. He said alright and hung up. Right when I hung up with Stephon Ms. D called.

"What's good with you ma?" I answered.

"Well, we got the men where they need to be at."

"Cool, but did you remember to tell the women that it's gonna run em $100 an hour?" I asked.

"Yes," she replied.

"Good and thank you for today. Nigga needed that stress relief."

"I did too!" she said.

"Well I gotta be out, I gotta get this show."

After we said our goodbyes, I went to the kitchen to see what Sunni whipped up real quick. She knows I'm a simple nigga and I gotta ride out in a few, so she threw together grilled bologna, cheese with some BBQ chips on the side.

I washed my hands and sat down to eat. Sunni yelled for

Babygirl to come home, she skipped into the kitchen and sat down beside me.

Sunni gave us our plates and a bottle of water. While eating Babygirl asked, "Daddy, can I have a phone so I can talk to my friends?"

"I'll think about it, and how much is the phone you want?" I asked.

"In the paper it says $49, and it's a smartphone daddy," she replied.

"We'll talk about it tomorrow after I get home," I told her, and finished eating.

When I was done I went to finish getting ready. I went back to the kitchen. "Well, I'm out. This money ain't gonna make itself. Love ya'll and see you later." I kissed Babygirl on the forehead and gave Sunni a deep kiss before heading out.

I jumped in my ride and went to swoop up Gee before heading to the ville.

—·—

When I pulled up at Gee's spot, I texted him and let him know I was outside. He came out and jumped in a few minutes later. "Bout time nigga! I'm tryna grab me something to drink before the show jump off," I said.

"Damn bro, had to make sho my shit was straight. But I'm ready now though," Gee replied.

As I pulled off I thought about our next show that was coming up. "Aye bro, an older lady wants to book a show and wants us to dress like firemen. Is that cool with you?" I asked.

"Yeah, that's straight, because the cop routine is kinda old and played out."

"Remind me to get Ms. D's number put on the card, because they are getting paid to help us," I told Gee. Finally pulling up to the liquor store, we went in instead of hitting the drive through.

"How're you officers doing tonight?" the clerk asked.

"We good, thank you," I replied. A nigga didn't like hearing that but I'm looking at the money that's coming with this. I grabbed me a Red Bull to go with my drink and Gee did the same with a bottle of Henny. We paid and I gave the clerk one more nod before walking out.

Outside the liquor store on Protho Junction in Lil Rock, the night air was cool, but still warm with a breeze. It was kinda packed on the north side of town, but we were on a mission so we headed to my BMW and hit 161 Highway to the 'Ville. I bumped that "100 Million" by DJ Khaled, Birdman, Jeezy, Ross and Weezy.

I turned the radio down so Gee could hear me when I told him to pour up and put some heat behind that gas. I grabbed my phone from the cup holder and called Karen to let her know we were on our way.

After I hung up, he handed me my cup and I turned the music back up and coasted to the 'Ville thinking that I was on my way. I thought about all the shit I'd get my daughter and Sunni. Gee passed me the blunt and I hit it hard and inhaled deep. As I released the smoke I instantly felt the effects of the gas. We finally hit Military Road in the 'Ville and we busted a right on Military heading toward Lumoke, and a few minutes on Military we were pulling up at Karen's house.

I put my cups down and I cut the car off. Gee had finished the blunt off and downed the rest of his Red Bull and Henny.

"You ready to get this paper my guy?" I asked.

"Hell yeah, that's what we out here for!" he said. I can tell my nigga was amped up and having fun. We could hear music blasting from inside the house. We got our shit together and headed toward the front door.

We got to the door and I rang the doorbell. After a couple minutes, I rang the doorbell again. This time it only took a few seconds for Karen to answer the door.

"Finally, it took you long enough" I told her, and she just smirked. We made small talk and Ms. Rose comes to the door.

"Can I help you officers?" she asked.

"We got a call about the music. Too many cars parked on the street," I told her.

"Sorry officers, we'll turn it down," she replied.

At the same time, Gee sniffed the air and said, "Is that weed I smell?"

"Sir, we just tryna kick it and chill. We don't want no problems," Ms. Rose said.

"Ma'am, can we step in for a minute and talk to you and your company?" I asked.

She took a deep breath and opened the door for us.

"If you don't mind me asking, how old is everyone here?" I asked.

"We're all over 21," Ms. Rose said with an attitude. We followed her to the living room and women were sitting around playing cards, talking shit, and being loud. Karen went and cut the music down.

"We got a disturbance call, I need to see some IDs," I said.

Everyone got to groaning in disapproval. A woman named Barbara handed me her ID first.

She was seated in a loveseat by herself, so I went to hand her back her ID, and that's when the music came back on. I gave a slight look back over my shoulder and smirked at Karen and snatched my shirt off and began throwing that dick in Barbara's face.

Barb was a thick ass sista. About 5'7", 160, and it was all in the hips, thighs, and ass. She had shoulder length hair, paper sack brown skin that gave off a glow, and light brown eyes.

She was a sexy ass woman at 30. She threw her hands up and smiled real big as I snatched my pants off, showing off a pair of Ralph Lauren boxer briefs. Then I noticed the women started reaching for their billfolds. They fired that gas back up. When I looked over at Gee he got Karen on the floor grinding into her so good that the grey leggings she had on was wet between her legs when he finally let her up.

I pulled Rose off the sofa's arm, took the blunt, hit it, and inhaled deeply while slowly grinding my semi-erect dick in her face. She noticed it and began running her hand up and down my length. I didn't mind women getting they feel on sometimes, they came outta pocket more if they see a lil more.

I blew the smoke out and pushed her onto the sofa and stood up on it and grinded more into her face. She put her face deep into my crotch, biting my dick, and I wasn't tripping, we all was high and a lil tipsy and feeling ourselves.

When that "Strip for You" by R. Kelly went off they turned the music down a little bit and Rose spoke up.

"Can ya'll stay and fuck wit us tonight? We'll give ya'll an extra hunnid a piece."

"I don't know ma, I gotta get home," I told her.

"We just want ya'lls company that's all," she slurred. One of the women that we didn't catch her name grabbed her purse and said she had to get home to her kids and husband. By the time we got done at this party it was after 2:30AM on Tuesday morning, and I thought to myself, *Damn, we just getting started and we still got a lot of parties to go.*

We gave the ladies hugs, got dressed, and headed out.

"When ya'll gonna be available again?" Rose asked.

"Shit, Karen knows how to get in touch," I told her, and I closed the house door behind me and Gee.

As we got in my car I just caught my phone ringing. I looked at the screen to see Sunni's name, then Gee's phone started ringing too.

"Damn, ya wife blowin' you up too?" I asked Gee jokingly. He laughed and answered his phone when I told him to put one in us on the way to the house. I drove as Gee rolled up and talked to his wife. He fired it up and passed it to me.

I took a few hits and inhaled deeply, instantly feeling the effects from that pressure. We passed the blunt back and forth and by the time we made it to Gee's spot, we'd rolled up and smoked a half before Gee put it out, gave me some dap, and we parked behind his truck to split the money.

When we cut on the dome light and came outta pocket, we noticed 20s and 50s.

"Them hoes had to have been throwed bro, this about a stack and some change!" I said excitedly. It was $1600 and some loose dollas. It was about ten to fifteen women in the house, some we didn't catch their name.

"I'ma catch up with you lata homie," Gee said, getting out and closing the door. I killed the dome light, put my car in reverse and left Gee's.

Then I texted Sunni and told her, *I'm on my way home.*
She replied, "Ok."

I fired up the other half of the blunt and cranked that "Your Bodies Callin'" by R. Kelly and enjoyed the rest of my drive home.

—•—

Pulling up in the driveway it was around 4am. I packed, locked up my car, and headed in the house, pocketing my money. Unlocking the door and going in, locking it behind me and kicking off my shoes at the door, I could hear the TV on in the living room. But Sunni wasn't in there so I went to check on Babygirl, who was still asleep. I closed her door and headed to the bedroom. Sunni was coming out the bathroom. I dropped my uniform shirt in the chair in the corner of the room and flopped on the bed, pulling everything out my pockets.

"Damn, bae, looks like ya'll made a killing tonight!" she exclaimed, grinning.

"Yeah, it was a houseful, but some of that is from earlier too," I replied.

"Bae, don't forget about Babygirl's phone?"

"I ain't forget. Get a hunnid out for her and another for her plan and stuff. Put the rest into our savings," I told Sunni.

"How did it go at your brother's house?" she asked, sitting down on the bed next to me. I let her lay her head on my chest and enjoyed the feeling of having a good woman by my side who cared about my business.

"It's all coming along," I told her. "We got sites set up, our name is getting out there, the women are already hitting us up for shows. Ms. D got me stressed though," I said, frowning.

"Why? What she do?"

"She was pressing pretty hard for me to keep my money at Lil Jon's place. Said he got a safe there. But I don't want my cash anywhere near where his business was set up."

"That's a good idea bae."

"D said he had all the dope taken when he was arrested, but if someone comes looking around I don't know what they'll find. Better to have the money over here with us where I know for sure it's safe."

"I know it's been helping you to have his business associates get involved and run some shit for you, but be careful E. Just cause they know your brother doesn't mean they're good company. Anyone who wants to take money outta your hands is suspicious."

I agreed with her and felt better about my decision.

It was 4:41 AM, so me and Sunni had been up talking for a lil minute. I decided to take a shower in the morning. I was too high, tipsy, and tired to get up.

"Ma, I'm outta there, I need some sleep," I told Sunni. She put the money in the nightstand, hit the lights, and cuddled up to me. Instantly I was in a cold sleep and dreaming of a good night replaying in my head.

6

WHEN I ROSE LATER THAT day to the sun shining in my face, music playing softly in the living room and the smell of food woke me up faster. "Damn, dis don't feel like a Tuesday morning," I groaned.

Getting up, I headed to the shower before going to see what Sunni and Babygirl had jumping in the kitchen. I got in the shower and turned it on as hot as I could stand it. Because of hitting the gym and doing last night's show, I was aching and bone tired.

I lathered up a few times with my Axe body wash and rinsed off and let the water roll over my freshly shaved bald head, because I did have a slight migraine.

After a quick 15 minutes I turned the water off, grabbed my big red drying towel, and wrapped it around my waist. I brushed my teeth and hit my grill with some mouthwash and slid on my muscle shirt, boxers and Jordan shorts Sunni must've laid out for a nigga. She kept this up, she was going to have a nigga spoiled to death.

I headed back into our bedroom to get some socks before stepping to the kitchen. I hit myself with a lil squirt of cocoa butter lotion first.

Making it into the kitchen, Sunni was at the stove and Babygirl was sitting down doing something on Sunni's tablet.

"Good morning bae," I said, putting some excitement in my voice, not trying to sound down because deep inside I wanted to still be sleeping.

I kissed my daughter on the forehead and wrapped my arms around Sunni.

"Mmmm...good morning bae," I said as I hugged her from behind.

"Good morning or good afternoon daddy," Sunni replied.

"What smells so good?" I asked, sitting beside Babygirl and tugging one of her pigtails.

"Um...some oven baked BBQ chicken, fried potatoes with grilled chopped onions and green beans."

"Damn it sho smells good cause I'm hungry as hell!" I told her. She just laughed.

"So, what's planned for tonight?" Sunni asked.

"Well, we got a small show tonight...matter of fact, where my phone?" I asked.

"In the living room on the charger," she said. I got my phone and returned to the kitchen. Looking at it, I had missed calls from a couple of the fellas and Ms. D's spoiled ass. I called AB. He answered on the third ring, "What's good E?"

"Not shit man, I got a little paper for ya'll, so go pick up Sam and head to my spot," I told him.

"Alright, bet that," he said, and hung up.

I texted Raheem and told him too, but he didn't respond back, so that young nigga was probably still sleeping.

Ms. D called again right as Sunni sat me and Babygirl's food in front of us.

"What's good ma?" I answered.

"How'd it go last night?"

"It was straight, I got a little paper for you and the girls," I told her.

"E, I'm straight, you need to be saving right now, and if the fellas was on your team, you need to explain to them what's up."

"Yeah, you right. I'll schedule a meeting for this weekend to see who's gonna stay and who's gonna walk."

"Alright, well get at me."

"Cool, I'ma stop by tonight," I told her.

"Oh, and we got a few tonight. An Ann Webb in South West, Shonequa Jones in the North, and Joyce in Jacksonville."

"Alright, text me they info, cause I'm sitting down eating with my family right now."

"Okay. Talk to you later." And with that she hung up. I dug into my food alongside Babygirl.

—•—

After we ate, I grabbed my phone and went back to our bedroom. A few minutes later Babygirl came in and sat on the bed beside me.

"Well how do you like your new phone?" I asked her, because I seen the text message from Sunni saying she was taking Babygirl to get her phone that morning. "Thank you daddy! I can't wait to show my friends," she said excitedly.

"Now, we gotta get you some kinda duties where you can keep ya bills paid," I told her. Then Sunni came walking in the room. "Thank you babe for that good homecooked meal," I told her. She just answered me by giving me a kiss and kissing Babygirl's forehead.

"Going to take a shower, bae," she said, and disappeared into the bathroom.

"Go play with your friends Babygirl. Daddy's got some stuff to handle."

"Okay," she said, and run out the room.

A few minutes later she popped back up at the door.

"Some men are at the door," she said with a concerned look on her face.

"Tell them to wait in the living room Babygirl. And thank you," I told her. She skipped along to relay the message.

I got up and told Sunni we had company before I stepped into the living room. "What's good with ya'll?" I said, stepping in and giving Sam, AB, Stephon, and Raheem some dap.

"Man, not too much of shit, came to drop this bread off, and ol'girl said you wanted to holla at us?" AB said.

So Ms. D wanted me to go ahead and talk to them now and see who was down and who wasn't.

"Yeah, a nigga was gonna wait until Friday. But fuck it. Man, I know ya'll worked hard these last few days or so, and I'm thankful for that," I said, and continued, "but as ya'll know I'm still tryna save to get us a club, and if ya'll help me build this empire, I'll make sure ya'll get well taken care of." I waited to see the outcome.

AB slapped 3 stacks on the table. "Big man we down, because I know I like this shit and the otha's ain't complaining," he said, and the rest of them shook their heads.

"Aight, cool. I'ma text ya'll the same message of three names and addresses so pick where ya'll want to go and handle that. Those are booked for tonight too," I told them. "Handle that and get back at me later tomorrow." I was going to give them a few days off to get some rest and chill with they fam and do they thing. "Ya'll just make sho ya'll on point, and the customers are happy. Unhappy customers are bad for business," I told them, walking to the living room door.

They gave me some dap before heading out. I walked back

to our room and Sunni was putting on lotion and getting ready to go run around and handle some business. "Do you need some bread to spend ma?" I asked.

"Nah daddy, I'm good. I'm just handling some small shit and coming back home."

"Aight, well get me a stack out just in case," I told her. She went to our stash in the closet and came out with a rubber band roll of money.

"Thank you, ma," I said. "Gotta make some calls, but text or call if you need anything," I told her, heading into the living room to call Gee and Ms. D.

I called Gee first, he answered after a few rings.

"What's good, E?"

"Not shit man, just hittin' you to come pick up your paper."

"Nah E, throw that in the pot homie. Ms. D already told me what's up and you got a rida in me too," he replied.

"I know, I appreciate it bro, I'm ready to get this club jumpin'."

"Gotta have patience my nigga," he replied

"Well, we might hit the next scene as firemen."

"That's cool too bro."

"Bet, well I'ma get up with you once I leave the house. Remember, we got that show tonight, and we won't pick back up until Friday."

"Alright, bet I'll see you in a minute," he said, and we disconnected.

"Bae, I'm out, I'll see you later, and I texted you Babygirl's number too," Sunni said, kissing me and heading out the door. My eyes followed that ass and her skintight jeans looked like they were painted on.

When I went to our room and got ready to go get Gee,

texting Babygirl to ask would she be okay until Sunni g
ot back to the house. She simply replied *Yep*. So I locked the
door even though she was next door. Loaded up and headed
to get Gee.

I pulled out the driveway and cranked my stereo up bumping that "All My Bitches Got Friends" by Miguel. We already
had our costumes for tonight. All we had to do was dress up
and pull up.

As I made it to pick up Gee, like always it took this nigga a
minute to come out the house. This nigga acted like a woman
when it came to him getting ready for these shows and it was
only 6:40 PM, and we still had to stop at D's house before we
go to the party.

He came out to the car finally. "Damn nigga! Why it always take you so long to come out?" I asked, playing.

"Man, I had to double check my gear," he responded.

"Aye, after we get this rolling, I'm thinking about getting a
magazine started to go with our club scene. What you think?"

"That's straight too. It'll give the females locked up something to look at and extra money to come it."

"Alright! It's good to have the support," I told him, pulling
out and heading to North Little Rock to Ms. D's spot.

Gee fired up that gas as we headed to the North in
Glenview. We stopped at Protho's Liquor to get a bottle of gin
and orange juice.

That old school shit, I thought as we drove the last five minutes to Ms. D's.

When we got there I parked behind her car but couldn't
really tell if Kim and Tana was there or not. We finished our
dranks and the blunt before we headed inside the house. When
we walked in Kim was on the couch on her phone. She got real
quiet as soon as we walked in.

"What's up ma? Where's everybody at?" I asked her.

"Tana gone and D's in her room," she replied.

Gee dropped on the couch beside Kim and I headed to the back room. I tapped on her door and waited.

"Come on," she said. "Oh, what's good E? I thought you wasn't coming until later?"

"Well, a nigga didn't have shit to do until later. What's up with you?" I asked as my phone began to vibrate in my pocket. I looked at it when D walked into the bathroom to finish putting on some clothes. Her hair was wet so you can tell she was fresh out the shower.

AB texted saying that they gonna be in South West at a female named Ann Webb's, that Kim said hit her up on Facebook.

"Mmmm, so you just decided to come see me?" D asked, coming out the bathroom in some booty shorts that said Sissy on the ass, and a matching muscle shirt.

"Damn, what now, I can't come see you?"

"Nah, I ain't saying that, I was just asking," she said, walking up on me all seductive and shit.

"Alright cool, I just wanted to tell you all dem niggas on board. They ready to build this empire with me."

"Good. So you can save every dime and we can begin our tours," she said, and stood on her tiptoes to kiss me. I palmed dat ass and deepened the kiss, listening to her moan. When I broke the kiss she grabbed a handful of dis dick and drew a groan from me.

"When can I have some more of daddy's dick?" she asked.

"Maybe later if I ain't too tired and fucked up," I replied.

"Okay, bet."

"But I gotta be out, I gotta go handle some more shit," I said, and gave her a little slap on that ass.

"Okay, just text me."

"Bet," I said, walking into the living room.

Gee and Kim was hugged up watching TV.

"You ready to roll teddy bear ass nigga!" I said, looking at him cuddled up on Kim.

"Yeah nigga, alright," he said, Kim pinching a nigga on the ass. I just laughed and walked out to my car.

My phone went off again. It was a text from Sam saying they are going to the Bluff to a female named Joyce Smith's. So that left me and Gee in the North.

We stopped by the liquor store to get some more ice and OJ for our gin. When I pulled up and got out, upon walking in the store I saw a familiar face, and I approached the nigga.

"Yo BG! What's good with you homie?" I asked.

"Man! What's good Big E, it's been a while since I seen you."

"Yeah man, what's been up with you bruh?"

"Not shit fam, just got out, now a nigga looking for a job to keep those folks off my ass."

"Cool. Speaking of a job, I can use a nigga of your caliber and size on my team."

"And what you got going, E?"

"Man, I started my own business of male strippers."

"Yo! I never heard of that shit down here," he said, then my phone began to go off.

"Man here's my card, just get at me if you looking to put some paper in ya pocket."

"Bet." And we dapped before I grabbed my ice and juice and headed to my ride.

Answering the phone, I seen Babygirl's name across my screen.

"What's up Babygirl?" I said.

"Dang daddy, you must got my number programmed?" she asked.

"Yeah, gotta keep up with my baby," I replied.

"Wassup daddy?"

"Just checking on you and making sho everything aight at the house."

"Yeah we good. Sunni said she don't feel good, so she laying down."

"Okay, keep me informed on how she doing and you make sho you beat them streetlights home," I told Babygirl.

"Okay," she said and disconnected our call.

I turned up McCain and headed to the next show, because it was already getting late and this woman was probably wondering where a nigga at. I grabbed my phone out the cup holder and sent Shonequa a text letting her know I was down the way, and she replied *Damn! Finally. I thought a bitch got beat! Nah ma, we about ten minutes out,* I told her.

—•—

After bustin' a couple corners in Lakewood Village, I thought to myself, *Damn, a nigga gotta get a spot like this.* As I turned down the music Gee looked up from his phone.

"Damn E! Where we at? These houses look expensive as fuck," he said.

"Yeah they do, but we still in the North in Lakewood Village," I said, looking at the numbers on the brick built mailboxes to make sure I don't miss lil mama spot, but I didn't have to look too much, because I spotted a house on Lakewood Circle in the cul-de-sac with a lotta cars out front and in the driveway.

I pulled behind a black on black Challenger in the cul-de-sac. The house was two-tone red brick bottom and white wood panel top, and it was a two-story spot. I killed the lights.

"Damn, we might hit the payload here, E," Gee said

excitedly. Downing the rest of our drinks and popping the trunk so we can get our firemen's gear on and stepping out, I smelled BBQ, so I knew they was kicking it tough.

"Yeah, they jamming bro, let's get this bread man!" I told Gee.

"Hell yeah, with all these nice ass cars bro, we need to be leaving with some real paper and not no change," Gee replied.

"I agree."

Grabbing our fire axes and helmets before making our way to the front door, I asked him, "Ready?" He just nodded and gave me some dap as I rang the doorbell. We waited.

About 30 seconds later Shonequa answered the door looking sexy as fuck. This was my first time meeting her face to face, and the bitch was bad. At 5'7", light skin complexion with light brown eyes, she was thick as hell and had nice titties. She came to the door wearing some black booty shorts, a plain white v-neck, red ankle socks.

"Can I help you?" she said, sounding country as hell.

"Yes ma'am, someone called and reported to be smelling smoke," I replied.

"Now ain't nothing burning over here, but a BBQ grill smokin'!" she said with a smart-ass mouth.

"Well this is #19 Lakewood Circle?"

"Yeah but didn't nobody call the fire department ova here. You know it was prolly dese nosy ass neighbors!" she said.

I noticed she had a red dixie cup in her hand.

"Well ma'am, we still have to conduct our inspection and verify everything ourselves if you don't mind."

"But I said ain't nothing smokin but a grill!" she said with an attitude.

"Ma'am, we're just doing our job, that's it. We'll do our inspections and be done," Gee said. After a few seconds she finally broke.

"Damn! Alright, but I'm trying to enjoy my birthday so could ya'll hur-up!" she groaned.

"Yes ma'am," I replied. She and a few of her friends stepped to the side and let us in.

"Damn," I heard one of them say.

"Dis way!" Shonequa said, and we followed her through the house. I set my axe down by the door and Gee followed suit. When we made it to the back of the house, she directed us to where everybody was kicking it at. We reached the back patio.

"See, no fire!" she said, kinda slurring her words.

"Okay ma'am. We're sorry for the misunderstanding," I said, walking back toward the living room where it was about twenty maybe thirty women were all sitting around a coffee table playing Tonk and drinking and some sitting around dancing and talking.

"Fireman" by Weezy was coming on.

"You smell that Gee?" I asked.

"Yeah," he replied.

"I don't smell shit!" Shonequa said.

"I smell a fire!" I told her, standing in the doorway of the living room.

"I don't!" she said.

"And it's in my pants!" I yelled and snatched off my jacket and pulled off my button-down-the-side pants. All the women jumped up from the table and went crazy. There was all shapes and sizes got to grinding on me from the front to the back. Gee was right on cue, and the women got even louder.

"Damn!" Shonequa said as I pulled her to me and ground on her and spun her around and pulled dat ass to my dick. As she threw her hair back and looked over her shoulder in a standing doggy style move I ground on her hard, making sure she felt my semi hard dick all on dat ass.

The other women just stood back as I had their friend and birthday girl's ass tooted up in the air working her up good. I look over to see Gee got this red bone on the love seat. He was standing wearing some tight boxer briefs thrusting his dick in her face. She had red hair and freckles to match and she was tatted up. I lay Shonequa down on her floor and ground on her some more as I felt hands on my ass and waist band.

I knew they'd begun sliding money down my shit.

"Ya'll gonna make a nigga put in some work huh?" I said, outta breath.

"Hell yeah!" Shonequa said.

"Aight bet!" I accepted the challenge and pushed her down on the floor on her hands and knees, continuing the same grinding motion while she was still in doggy style.

"Damn, nigga! You keep that up I'ma pay for more than a dance!" she growled, looking back over her shoulder. I let her up and went to dance on some of the other women so Shonequa could take a break. When I looked over at Gee, my nigga was sweating like crazy and enjoying hisself.

The ladies was making it rain like a real strip club in this mu'fucka. I looked at the clock over by this big ass flat screen and it was a little after 11:30 PM. So I gave the rest of the night my all and collected my money in the process.

—•—

By the time I looked at the clock again it was Wednesday — 3 AM.

Damn, the time flew by! I thought to myself. I looked over at my dude and he was still kickin it, but the crowd had gotten kinda thin.

Gee made eye contact with me and I gave him that nod, like 'yeah, it's time to go.' I got dressed as he finished up his last little dance, picked up the money he made, and got dressed too.

Shonequa came over to walk me to the door and we made small talk on the way over there. She told me she writes articles for a magazine and I asked her could I call her sometime because I've got ideas for my own magazine and I'd like her input on it.

Gee caught up with us. "Don't be a stranger, ma," I told her as we headed to my whip. As we loaded up our shit, I got in and fired up the car. I sat back and thought about my business and the next step I was going to take. Meeting Shonequa felt like fate. Everything was going right.

"Aye, bruh, I'm really done with this shit. I'm going to sit back and run this shit. What you gonna do fam?" I asked Gee as he settled into the passenger seat and rolled a blunt for the ride home.

"Shit homie, I'm straight. I kinda like throwing da dick in dese females faces to get dat bread. I'll do it a lil longer then I'll shut it down," Gee said.

"Cool, because that'll give me a chance to get more help by the time you get ready to fall back," I told him.

"Alrighty," he said, laying back, putting some heat to the blunt as we pulled outta lil mama's drive and headed back to drop him off before heading home myself.

——•——

An hour later, I was pulling up to the house and not a sign of life was present. I looked at the clock in my car and it was a little after 4 AM. Heading inside, the house was cool, and I could hear the living room TV on so either Sunni or Babygirl was up.

I dropped my stuff in the hallway closet and made my

way to the living room. Sunni was in the corner of the couch watching something on HBO.

"Hey bae, you hungry?" she asked when I dropped on the couch beside her.

"Yeah, but I wanna get a shower first, and might I ask what a beautiful thang like you doing up so early?" I asked.

"Couldn't sleep, so I figured I'd watch some TV until I fell asleep. But that didn't do any good. So how'd it go tonight?" Sunni asked, snuggling in close to me.

"It was alright. A lil moe packed than it was last time, but so far so good," I replied.

"That's good bae. So what's new?"

"Don't know yet, but I think tonight was my last show," I told her.

"What's wrong bae?" she asked with a concerned look on her face.

"Nothing. I just wanna sit back and run my business, not work for it too," I told her.

"Oh, well that sounds bout right."

"Yeah, and the woman that threw the party well, come to find out she writes articles for a magazine and I think she can help me get mine started," I told Sunni.

"Cool. But go take a shower and we'll talk more when you get out and I get you fed," she told me, placing a kiss on my smooth shaved head. I watched her thick yellow ass stride to the kitchen.

"Damn, a nigga lucky," I said to myself as I headed to the bedroom to take a quick shower. On the way down the hall I peeped in on Babygirl and seen she was knocked out. I closed her door. In my room, I could see Sunni already had me a pair of shorts, boxers, and t-shirt ready.

—•—

After about 20 minutes of soaking in the hot water and Old Spice body wash, I dried off, dressed, and headed for the kitchen, where it smelled good.

"Damn ma, what you cooking? It smells like Waffle House in dis mu'fucka," I said to Sunni and walked up behind her to wrap her up while she was at the stove.

"Eggs, scrambled, with diced onions, bell peppers, hash browns with cheese on top and turkey sausage links," she replied.

"Bet dat up!" I told her, stomach touching my back.

"Bae, now what was you saying bout you working to get a magazine started?" Sunni asked.

"Well, I've got a few guys getting out the joint soon and I'ma give em a job, so I can generate some more money to help speed up the process of the club."

"That sounds like a good plan if you already got all ya ducks in a row."

"Yeah, I do kinda, just got some more shit I gotta work out and get together," I replied. She sat my plate of hot breakfast in front of me. She knew a nigga eats like a king.

"Thanks bae," I told her. She made her a plate and sat beside me and we blessed our food before digging in.

My phone went off in the living room where I had left it.

"Be right back," I told. Sunni. I made it in time to see why my phone was going off at 5:45 in the morning. It was a few messages from my guys letting me know they done and got dey bread. I texted them all the same shit letting em know to cash in later because I'm about to cash out for a few hours. It's a good thing we ain't started back up until Friday. Let everybody get some rest. Then I thought I gotta make time to hit the gym as I put my phone back on charger and go finish eating.

It was still hot and Sunni was done eating, just playing on her tablet waiting on me.

"Come to bed when you're done, I'll worry about the dishes later," she told me, kissing me on the cheek and heading to bed.

I got done with my meal, put my cup and plate in the sink, and headed to bed. Making it to the room, the alarm clock read 6:03 AM and I climbed into bed and listened to Sunni's light snoring. I cuddled up to her and within minutes of hitting my pillow, I was almost asleep, but I remembered to set the alarm to 11:45 before dozing off.

———•———

I was startled awake by Babygirl shaking me.

"Daddy! Get up! Something's wrong with Sunni!" she screamed in my face. Upon her saying that, I immediately jumped up and followed Babygirl into the living room where Sunni was curled up on the floor.

"Call 911 Babygirl!" I yelled. I picked her up and carried her back to the bedroom and laid her down until an EMT unit came. I hurried and got dressed, grabbing my keys as I heard Babygirl talking to someone. Seconds later a paramedic followed her into the room.

"How long has she been out?" the black woman with dreads asked.

"I don't know. Bout 15 minutes or so!" I said as they put her onto a gurney and rolled her out to an ambulance. "Come on Babygirl, get your stuff!" I yelled and we rushed out the door behind them. Me not forgetting my phone, I called Kay and asked her to meet me at the hospital to get Babygirl, and I'd come get her later. She agreed and we jumped in my 745 and trailed the ambulance to the hospital.

Sunni

I woke up to bright lights in my face. Everything so bright, and I'm hearing all this beeping and shit around me. I tried to sit up and open my eyes and felt a pair of hands on my shoulders.

"Woah, Ms. Gibson, you took a nasty fall and got a mean bump on your forehead," a deep voice said. I opened my eyes and they finally adjusted to the light. That's when I realized I was in a hospital room, and instantly fear took over. I shot up.

"Ms. Gibson take it easy!" he said. "You don't want to put anymore strain on your baby," he added.

"Baby?" I said with a concerned look on my face.

"Yes, you're four weeks pregnant," he replied, and exited the room. I laid back rubbing my stomach thinking about the new life I was about to bring into this world. Tears began to cloud my eyes. I closed my eyes and began to daydream about all the possibilities of what my baby would be like.

Big E

As I sat in the waiting area, the short white balding man that told me to wait while he checked on Sunni came back out. He approached me and I had a million different things running through my head.

"Hey, sorry for rushing out like that, but I had to tend to that call. You're here for Ms. Gibson, am I right?" he asked, and I just nodded. "Well, she's doing okay. Took a nasty bump on the head but she'll be fine. You can come back to see her if you'd like."

I followed him through the double doors into the emergency area. I hadn't been to HAMS since I'd gotten shot some years ago. Everything was different. Doctors and nurses were rushing around everywhere. He directed me into the room and I saw Sunni laying back with an ice pack on her head, eyes closed, and still looking beautiful as ever despite the big ass bump on her head.

"Sunni? Bae are you alright?" I asked. Her eyes slowly fluttered open and I could see the tears waiting up in them. "What's wrong ma?" I asked and moved to sit on the bed beside her. She was still wearing her pink sweats and t-shirt she had on that morning and her pink and black Jordan's.

"I'm going to be a momma E!" she said and began to cry as I held her.

"Bae, that's okay, we're going to make sure he or she has the best of everything," I told her as she cried into my chest. At this little moment the doctor came back in holding a small paper cup and a clear cup of water.

"Here's something for your headache Ms. Gibson, and to introduce myself properly, I'm James Banks. I'll be your OBGYN for the remainder of your pregnancy," he said. We both nodded. "So make sure you get some rest and pick up some prenatal vitamins, and try to tackle less stressful tasks," he added and handed Sunni her release papers. He smiled and left us alone to get ourselves together.

The paper read that she had to come in for a monthly checkup. I put my hoodie on her, grabbed my keys and phone, and we made our exit.

"Where's Babygirl bae?" she asked.

"At Kay's, but you just need to worry about getting some rest. We'll tell her later," I replied. On the elevator ride down I thought to myself, *This is another reason to be home with Sunni.* We left the hospital and headed for the car to pick up Babygirl and go home.

In the car Sunni put on my sunglasses and let the seat back as we drove to John Barrow. I called Kay to deliver the news and she answered on the first ring, "What's good bro? Is every-thing okay?" she asked.

"Yeah, she's fine. They said she just tired and on top of that she's four weeks pregnant," I replied. "Let me tell Babygirl, Kay," I added.

"Bro, that's not my place, but you go ahead and take her home. I'll bring Babygirl home. I've already fed her too," she said.

"Alright, bet I'll meet you at her house," I responded and we disconnected our call.

We rode back to Dumas and I thought, *We really gotta move closer to the city.* On the way outta Little Rock I stopped at McDonald's and got something to eat and Sunni a small M&M McFlurry just to see how her stomach would take to it. I added some chicken selects, a grilled chicken sandwich and two large fries. After I paid for our food at the window and pulled off Sunni woke up. "You hungry ma?" I asked.

"Yeah, a little, thank you babe," she replied. She dug right into the chicken strips and BBQ. I reached for my chicken sandwich, which she handed to me while we headed outta Little Rock back home.

About 45 minutes later, we were pulling up to the house and Kay's Tahoe was in the driveway. I parked beside it, col-lecting the trash as Sunni was finishing her ice cream. Walking through the front door Babygirl must have sensed us because she came running out the living room into my arms.

"Daddy! Is Sunni okay?" she asked with tears in her eyes.

"Yes Babygirl, I'm fine," Sunni answered, coming in be-hind me. "I was just tired. Didn't mean to scare you like that." Kay came into the hallway as we rounded the corner with me holding Babygirl. She hugged me and hugged Sunni really tight and smiled big.

"Are you good son?" Kay asked.

"Yeah I'm good, jut tired," she replied.

"Well bae go lay down. I gotta place a few calls then I'll be in there to lay down with you," I said, putting Babygirl down. I headed outside to call Gee to tell him the news and see if the nigga would go pick up that bread from the fellas.

"What's good homie?" he answered on the 2nd ring.

"Not shit bruh, just got back from the hospital with Sunni. I'm about to be a father again!" I told him, thinking bout the time I missed with Babygirl.

"Dat's what's up fam. Congrats. But let me go gather this bread and I'ma swing by when I do."

"Aight," I replied and hung up. I went back inside where Kay and Babygirl was watching TV. I popped a squat beside Babygirl and pulled her closer to me, and I asked her, "You okay now?"

"Yeah, just glad Sunni's okay," she replied, sounding tired.

"Yeah, she was just tired, but she's okay now."

"Well E, I'm bout to head out and I'll fuck with you later," Kay said, hugging me and kissing Babygirl before going out the door.

"I'ma go lay down for a minute. Let me know if someone knock on the door," I told Babygirl before heading to the bedroom. When I get in my room, Sunni was curled up under the blanket facing the wall snoring softly. I kick my Jordan's off and crawled under the blanket up to her.

When I looked at the clock it was a little past 1 in the afternoon, and before I knew it I too was in a cold sleep.

—•—

"Daddy, somebody at the door!" I heard Babygirl yell. It was a little after 4:30 PM and Sunni was still out like a light. I get up to see who it is. When I made it in the living room I seen Babygirl talking to Gee.

"What's good bruh?" I asked.

"Man not shit, I went and got them pickups for you fam and the fellas wanna know wassup," he replied.

"I'ma let em know what it's looking like Friday. With me having another bun in the oven, I gotta work extra hard now," I told Gee, talking over Babygirl's head.

"Hell yeah, and with the team you building, we're gonna have our empire in no time. We just gotta stay down," Gee said.

"Yeah, I'ma do that," I told him as he handed me an envelope that was kinda thick.

"Feels good and thick homie?" I said.

"Yeah, but peep this, I gotta handle some more shit. You know to call or text if you need me," Gee said as I walked him to the door.

After closing and locking the front door I went back to the living room with Babygirl and she was playing on her phone.

"What's up lil girl?" I said, dropping beside her on the couch.

"Nothing! Can I go to my friends for a little while?" she asked.

"I don't see why not, just make sure you answer your phone when I call, and if ya'll go anywhere let me know," I told her. She jumped up, hugged me, and jetted for the door. Just as the front door closed Sunni walked into the living room, still looking tired.

"Where everybody go bae?" she asked.

"Bae just left and Gee and Kay went home," I responded.

"What's in that envelope?"

"Just a lil bread the fellas made during they shows. Gotta put it in the safe."

"You ain't gonna count it first?" she asked.

"Nah, I will later, but for right now I just wanna chill with you for a minute," I told her. "But first I gotta make a phone call before I do anything else," I added, getting up to find my phone.

When I got into our room I made my way to the safe in the closet. I had a few stacks of cash, but I still had some bread I had to stack and I was a long way off my mack. I put the brown envelope on top of everything else, making a mental note to count it later. Closing the safe and putting the wall panel back in place, I shut the closet and dialed up Ms. D to check on some shit. She answered after the 2nd ring.

"Wassup E?"

"Not shit ma, just called to check on some shit. Did a nigga named BG call?" I asked.

"Not that I know of but when he does, I'll let you know."

"Okay, bet, just call me when he does," I told her and headed back to the living room.

"You good ma?" I asked Sunni where she was curled up in the corner of the couch watching The Real.

"Yeah, just chillin' watching these hoes gossip," she replied, and I just laughed.

I sat beside bae and she laid her head in my lap.

"So, you done with your business? Can you chill with me now?" she asked.

"Of course, I'm through, just checking on one more thing and I can do that here with you," I responded, grabbing her tablet. I looked to see when my dudes JD and Shoe were getting out the pen, because right about now, I needed they help. JD got out in 3 weeks on June 11th and Shoe got out on July 3rd. That was perfect timing.

I'd have more help in less than two months.

"Who are they?" Sunni asked.

"Some fellas I fucked with in lock up that I promised a job to when they got out," I told her.

"Oh that's rad," she responded, and went back to watching TV.

"So what are you hoping for, because I want a lil Evan Jr.," I told her.

"Whatever you want bae, I'm satisfied with," she said, not taking her eyes off the TV. My phone started vibrating. I pulled it out and read the text message: *That guy called and said he needs a job,* Ms. D said.

Okay, bet and make sure you get the guys the info to they next jobs, I replied.

Ok.

I'ma drop by and holla 'atcha tomorrow, I sent.

"Yeah, bae, I can sit back and arrange some shit now, I got three more niggas trying to be down with the team," I told Sunni.

"Do I know em?" she asked.

"Prolly not, they neva went to the hole, so nah," I told her. The doorbell rang and I got up to get it. Answering the door, it was Mrs. Gibson, Sunni's mom.

"Hey mama, what brings you down this way?" I asked.

"Just come out to see my daughter and see if you'd let me get to know Babygirl better," she said, coming into the house, heading to the living room.

"Hey mama, whatchu doing here?" Sunni asked.

"Damn, I can't come check on my daughter?" she asked, getting offended.

"Now mama I'm just surprised to see you."

"Aw, I thought so. Where's Babygirl? I wanna take her for a little grandmother granddaughter time."

"She across the street way with her friends, I'll text her and get her over here," I said, going for my phone. After I sent the text a couple minutes went by and the front door opened again.

Babygirl appeared at the entrance of the living room.

"Wassup daddy?" she asked, coming to sit by me.

"You wanna go stay with Grandma G for a couple nights or just for the night?" I asked her.

"Yup, I'll go pack my stuff!" she said excitedly, jumping up and running to her room.

"What's ya'll plans, Mama G?" I asked.

"Ain't no tellin. Whatever my young soul brings to me to do. We'll probably go shopping. Cool, watch movies," she said. After about 30 minutes Babygirl came back in the living room with her Nike duffle.

"I'm ready!" she said, out of breath.

"You got your charger?" I asked, and she nodded. "Keep your phone on at all times lil girl," I said sarcastically.

"I will daddy, dang!" she said with a playful attitude.

They headed for the door with me on their heels. "Call me if you need anything Babygirl," I said as they waved bye and got in Ms. Gibson's Infiniti SUV. I headed back to the living room, where Sunni just looked at me funny.

"What up bae?" I asked.

"You didn't say nothing did you?" she asked.

"Nah, cause dat ain't my place. I figured you'd tell her when the time is right," I shot back to her.

"Okay, I'ma go lay back down. I don't feel good," she said, and headed for the room.

"I'll be in there in a few," I said, watching her disappear around the corner. I pulled out my phone and dialed up Gee. He answered before it went to the answering machine.

"What's good E?" he asked.

"Did you get that info from D about where we supposed to be going?" He repeated it to me. "Aight, cool. I talked to Sunni and told her I'm going to be stepping back and letting all these young men do the work," I told him.

"Yeah? Was she relieved? I know my baby mama can't wait for me to start supervising and stop dancing."

"Sunni knows what's up," I said. "She knows she doesn't need to worry about me straying on her."

"I don't know, man," Gee said cautiously. "All I'm gonna say is that usually when a woman isn't worried, it's because she's got one up on you."

"Nah man," I said, thinking about Sunni and the new life we were creating, "trust me, she loyal. Listen, meet me at the gym tomorrow round 1 o'clock and we'll talk about this next show," I told him.

"Bet," he said, hanging up.

I looked at my phone and it was a little after 8 PM and I wanted to look up a couple guys I fucked with back in the day before I got me some z's. I grabbed Sunni's tablet and headed to the room. When I get in the room she was out cold snoring and I thought to myself, *This is gonna be a long 9 months for bae.*

I climbed on my side of the bed, my side being closer to the door to shield her from any danger that might appear. I logged into Facebook and began looking up my homeboy back from my Oklahoma days named Carl Redman AKA Red. Within a few seconds into my search I found him and he still lived in OKC. I sent him a request, message, and tried to call him on Facebook, but got no answer.

I went through his pictures and he still into the same shit, now from the looks of it, he was turned his dream into a reality. My guy was a real pimp named Pimpin' Red. I logged out, set the tablet on the nightstand, and cuddled up to Sunni.

As she got under me and drifted deeper into sleep, I texted Gee and reminded him to meet me at the Planet Fitness in Little Rock at around 1 PM in the afternoon and killed the light and dreamed of my empire.

7

Raheem

THIS MALE STRIPPING SHIT WAS easy cash that a nigga could make besides the fact that I used to be a prison guard. I was really tired of seeing men, especially my own kind, caged up like animals. So it was time for me to find a new profession, and my guy Big E gave me the idea of becoming a male stripper.

Hell, I'd stacked me a little bit of bread before leaving the prison and I wasn't hurtin fo' shit, but I did have to keep my bread coming in if I wanted to keep my shit afloat. I sat thinking bout all this shit I had going for myself as I waited for my lil chick to come outta the waffle house with our breakfast.

I'd been lifting weights for the last couple years and I knew I had the body, tattoos, pearly whites and waves women would pay to see. At 5'11" I was what women considered a true Adonis.

A black Bentley pulled up beside my baby blue '86 Chevy Caprice on 28s. My car was nice and a classic, but looking at this Bentley, I knew it was time for me to upgrade the way I lived and what I rode in. A tall black man with a bald head and jewelry draped around his neck, waist, fingers, and it was a rose gold Rolex on his wrist.

He gave me a head nod as he passed my girl going in and her coming out.

Kei Kei only stood 5'1" and dark as chocolate, but she was bowed out and walked like a stallion. She had long black hair in braids, French tipped nails, some tight blue jean shorts, and a pink muscle shirt to compliment her thick fit frame, with some $200 Jordan's on her feet. She was down for a nigga for real. She climbed in the car and I cut my music down, bumping that "Colors" by Chief Keef.

"Damn Keisha, what took you so long? You been in there like an hour!" I said. I'm not one to raise my voice, but people knew how to take me serious.

"Damn bae, no thank you!" she said with an attitude.

"Sorry, ma. Thank you," I replied.

"Ya welcome, but this nasty black bitch fucked up my boo's omelet and hash browns so I made da bitch do da shit ova!" she said, smacking her lips.

"Well I do hope you didn't do nuttin crazy?" I said, looking at her sideways. I backed out of my spot and she didn't say a word as I pulled out into morning traffic in the bluff. My phone vibrated and it was a text from Gee letting me know to be at Planet Fitness at 1 o'clock later today. I didn't reply, just cut my music up and drove back to my lil 2-bedroom condo.

Big E

I woke up to the smell of breakfast being cooked. I looked at the clock and it was 9 in the morning. I felt a lot better after some good sleep. I jumped up, washed my face, hit my grill and headed to the kitchen.

When I walked in "Legs Shakin" by R. Kelly is playing softly on the small radio. Sunni had her hair in a ponytail that reached all the way to her luscious hips. Black booty shorts that said Pink on the back and a red t-shirt. She swayed to the music with her thick ass jiggling slightly. I walked up behind her and rubbed my semi-erect dick on her ass, and she gave a slight jump.

"Oh! Daddy you scared me," she said.

"I'm sorry, smells good bae," I said, rubbing my hand down the front of her shorts, parting her pussy lips.

"Don't start nothing you can't finish," she moaned.

"Oh I can finish, that's how you got a bun in the oven. But I gotta build some energy. A nigga hungry," I said, removing my hands from her shorts and getting me some juice before I sat at the table and listened to that R. Kelly.

She was cooking some beef sausage links, scrambled eggs with cheese, and pancakes. I was in deep thought she sat my plate down in front of me and took to the seat across from me.

"What you thinking bout Daddy?" she asked.

"You and the baby and how I'ma tell Babygirl," I responded.

"Well tell her baby, we just don't need to wait too much longer."

"Yeah, I know," I replied, digging into my breakfast and pouring syrup on everything.

"You eating for two now bae?" she said.

"Huh?" I said, looking up, and she began to laugh.

"I'm just playing daddy! Now eat!" she said, and I dug in.

After eating and helping Sunni straighten up the kitchen I went to get dressed and get my gym shit ready. I grabbed my duffle, keys, and phone and headed back into the living room where she was curled up on the couch watching TV.

"You need anything before I head out?" I asked.

"Nope, but can you get me some more ice cream before

you come back home bae?' she asked.

"What kind ma?"

"Cookie dough."

"Alright, I gotchu," I said, kissing her on the forehead and heading out. I looked at my phone once I got in my car and rolled down the windows to let some of the heat escape. It was 10:15 AM. I called T-Baby once I located her number. She answered on the third ring.

"Hellooooo," she moaned, sounding sexy and coming outta her sleep.

"What up ma? Did a nigga catch you at the wrong time?" I asked.

"Who is dis?"

"Dis Big E ma," I replied.

"Aww shit, what's up?" she said, sounding excited to finally hear from me.

"Who dat bae?" I heard a niggas voice in the background.

"My boss want me to come in later," she replied.

I thought to myself, *Damn dis bitch tells lies like it's natural. Hoes play games like men for real.*

"E, you there?" she came back on the phone.

"Yeah, I see I hit you at the wrong time. Hit me when you free and if you or your friends need some party entertainment, you got my number," I said, and hung up without giving her a change to reply. I pulled off and headed to the North Side to Ms. D's spot.

After a 30-minute drive I pulled up in Glenview. I noticed the black Jeep Wrangler with 28-inch Asanti's was in the driveway, so I knew Kim and Tana was home too. I parked behind the Jeep and headed in the house. Unlocking the door and stepping in, I noticed how quiet it was. Everyone was still asleep.

I headed to Ms. D's room and noticed the door was

cracked. I looked in and seen two bodies in her bed, and I felt a bit of jealousy but had to check myself because this wasn't my woman.

I closed the door and headed toward the den, where they had computers and shit set up. I sat behind the desk and woke the laptop up. They were still logged into Facebook and a couple more tabs were up for Instagram and Snapchat.

I clicked on Instagram and instantly a video started playing from when a nigga was at Shonequa's house a couple nights ago, and I thought to myself, *Damn, we kicked it that night.*

I looked through the pages for a minute before sending the computer back into sleep mode. I checked my phone for messages and had none, but it was going on 11 o'clock and hit me that I needed to hit Shonequa up about starting a magazine up. On my way out the door I gave her a call. She answered on the first ring.

"Helloo!" she said, sounding like I woke her up.

"Did I call at a bad time?" I asked.

"Who dis?"

"Dis Big E, ma. The one that did the lil show for you and ya homegirls."

"Oh, the one that told me bout wanting a magazine."

"Yeah, dat's me, but I didn't mean to wake you up ma," I said, trying to sound apologetic.

"Nah, it's good. Good morning."

"Good morning to you too, but is it okay if I swing through to holla at you if dat's aight?"

"Ummm…yeah. Sure it's time for me to get up anyways."

"Okay cool. Um, do you drink coffee or anything?" I asked.

"Yeah, I like my coffee like I like my men, strong and black," she replied, laughing.

"Well I gotchu ma. Give me a few and I'll be there." I

got in my 745 and headed toward McCain to Starbucks to grab coffee and breakfast for Shonequa. It was starting to heat up and it was only 11:07. I texted Gee and let him know to change the time of our gym meeting to 3 PM. He texted back a few minutes later and said *Bet*.

I hit him again and I told him to inform the guys of the time change.

I put on "I get Money" by 50 Cent and headed to my destination.

Shonequa

I was grinding my hips to the bed trying to enjoy my dream when the phone disturbed that, and I figured I needed to answer it because it could be my boss.

When I picked up, it was the guy who had stripped for my party. The man was sexy as hell and he turned me on bad. He wanted to talk about starting a magazine and he wanted my opinion on some things, which I don't know why he didn't wanna talk over the phone, but when he asked to come over and offered coffee, I said "Yeah," without a second thought.

I jumped up, hit the shower real quick, brushed my teeth. Looked over my naked body to make sure I didn't need to shave and thought *I'm not going to fuck this man, and he's just here on business. Hell, he probably gots a woman.* Then again... fuck it. I got needs too.

I lotioned my chocolate skin up with Johnson & Johnson baby lotion. I didn't use that other shit because I wanted to keep my skin soft as a newborn baby. I straightened up the bathroom, towel dried my hair, and ran a comb through it with some mousse and headed to my room to get dressed.

Considering the fact that I didn't have to report to an office, I worked from home, so I found me a pair of grey leggings that had Pink going across the ass and a t-shirt with Garfield on the front.

I didn't bother with panties or a bra because I was home working and I was sure I didn't have to go out anywhere. Everything I needed, I went and got the day before, but it was only Thursday so ain't no telling.

I slid on some gray and pink ankle socks and went to make sure the house was straight before Big E arrived. In the living room, it was okay but I still did a lil straightening up. I fluffed couch pillows and lit my vanilla scented Glade candles before grabbing my iPad glasses and throwing my still damp hair into a ponytail.

I sank to my favorite spot in the corner of the plush black loveseat and loaded up on my latest project. I was working on an article on woman's sexual stimulation and answering some questions from some of my followers. Deep in thought, the sound of the doorbell ringing made me jump. I gave everything a once over, pulled my ponytail tight and headed to the door.

I also gave myself a quick glance in the mirror before I opened the door. There stood one of the sexiest men I've ever laid eyes on. Big E was holding a cup holder from Starbucks loaded up with two coffees and a Starbucks bag. He had a freshly shaven head, tattoos shining under the early morning sun, and a crisp Nike t-shirt, shorts, and a pair of all white AirMax 90s. I couldn't help but lick my lips.

"Good morning," I said, letting him in.

Big E

I checked myself over as I waited for Shonequa to open the door. When she did, my mouth fell open slightly in admiration for her beauty. She looked like a real African goddess.

She had on a Garfield t-shirt that hugged her breasts and grey leggings that hugged her curved hips and thighs.

"Good morning," she said.

"Good morning to you too," I said as she stepped to the side, inviting me in.

"I hope you got an appetite because I got beef, sausage, eggs, and cheese bagels, and I hope you don't mind the beef, I don't eat pork," I told her.

"Nah that's cool, a bitch gotta watch her figure," she said, as we busted out laughing.

"I gotchu ma," I told her after I caught my breath. I followed her to the living room and noticed her spot looked good when she didn't have so many women and drinks and food everywhere. My eyes were glued to that ass and I knew my best bet was to go ahead and handle my business and get on down before I have her like I did the night of her party.

We took seats across from each other. I sat on the loveseat and she sat on the full coach. I passed her a coffee.

"Strong and black, huh?" she said when she looked at the side of the cup. I just cocked my eyebrow up at her. As I handed her the breakfast sandwich we began discussing my magazine.

"So do you have an editor or someone to print it?" she asked after I gave her the rundown about what my magazine would consist of and who it was marketed for.

"That's why I came to you."

"Okay. Hmmm...we gotta find you a photographer and group of editors and writers," she replied, finishing her sandwich.

"Well I want to put you in charge of getting all that together, and you can let me know what it's going to cost me," I responded, finishing my juice and sandwich.

"Okay. I got a guy in Cali I can call and I'll stay in touch," she told me.

"Aight, bet," I replied, checking the time, and it was just now turning noon.

"You got somewhere to be?" she asked.

"Yeah, in a few hours I gotta meet my team at the gym. Why, wassup?" I asked.

"Nun, no reason. I got some shit to handle too. Gotta finish writing this article for my magazine company."

"Cool, I really appreciate ya help, and thank you."

"No problem and thank you for breakfast."

"You welcome. I'ma get up out of here and let you get back to your article," I said. I rose off the couch and she walked me to the door. I couldn't help but lock onto that ass and from the looks of it, she didn't have no panties on. When I looked up we locked eyes and she gave me a slight smile, wink, and I knew then that I'd soon be fucking her, too.

"I'll be in touch," she said as she opened the door. I gave her a hug and my hands slid down her back and palmed that round ass. She gave me a soft moan.

"I'll be in touch soon, too," I said, and walked out the house into the noon heat.

I thought to myself, *I gotta fuck this woman!* Then I climbed in my 745 and headed back to Ms. D's house.

Ms. D

I guess he thought I was asleep when he peeked in my door and seen that I had a stranger laying in my bed. Hell, it was just a quick fuck, and he was supposed to leave after the dick he put on me, but we ended up having some drinks and I hit some of that fire ass weed he had and wanted to fuck again.

He wasn't a big time D-Boy but he got money. He was a couple years younger than me 37 years. He wasn't ugly, he was just a quick fuck. I didn't even know his name. I tapped his shoulder as he drooled on the pillow.

"Aye, it's time to go!" I said, wishing he was Evan. But he wasn't.

"Damn, you ain't offer a nigga breakfast! Just get the dick and put a nigga out," he complained, rolling over and snapping at me.

"Hell nah! Nigga you knew what dis was when I brought ya home!" I snapped back.

"Bitch! Ya pussy was bunk anyway," he said, getting his shit and heading for the door.

"Nigga, you one in all the niggas I fucked that thought so!" I told him, putting on my Victoria Secret all black with pink letters on it. He got dressed on his way out the door, but he knew better than to slam it.

"What's dat nigga's problem?" Tana said, with her pink hair tossed to the side, showing the designs on the shaved side.

"I put his weak tender dick ass out my bed and the nigga had the nerve to ask me to cook for him," I said, laughing.

"Was it that good?" Kim asked, bringing her thick ass in the kitchen.

"Hell nah, but he can eat some puddy though!" I said, slapping hands with Kim and Tana. They were my road dogs, and we been kicking it since pre-school.

"I'ma go get me a shower before Big E shows up," I said.

"Now that nigga got you dick drunk," Kim said, teasing me. But I kinda jumped on the defense.

"Bitch we just business partners!" I said with an attitude.

"Bitch calm down! I'm just playing!" she said, smiling.

"Oh well my bad," I said, leaving them laughing in the

kitchen. I stripped and jumped in the shower and thought about today's events.

Big E

As I pulled back up to Ms. D's spot, it was a little after 1 in the afternoon. So I knew she was probably up moving around. I was hoping that her boy toy was gone, because I'd hate to have to bust a nigga up for trying to play house and bow up to me. I parked behind the Jeep and got hit with that afternoon heat.

As I ascended the staircase the front door flew open and Tana brought her thick ass out the door.

"What's good ma?" I said. She looked up quickly.

"What's good E? D's in the shower," she said, going back to her phone, car keys in her hand.

"Aight. Aye, who's Jeep is that?" I asked.

"Something Kim's suga daddy bought her," she said.

"Shit! I'ma have to get me some fit fo a big nigga," I told her and she just laughed.

I walked into the living room and Kim was on the couch watching some type of game show. "Like the new Jeep ma. You gonna make a nigga upgrade," I said as she jumped a little bit.

"Damn it E! You scurred the shit outta me," she replied.

"Where D at?" I asked.

"Taking a shower. She should be out in a minute," Kim replied. Kim wasn't a top-notch bitch, but she could turn some heads with that ass she had and that silky black hair. As I eyed Kim, Ms. D popped up at the kitchen entrance.

"What's good E?" she asked, towel drying her hair.

"Not shit. What's been up witchu?" I shot back.

"Nothing. Tryna getcha business off da ground."

I nodded and she motioned me to the back room. I followed her with my eyes glued to that ass the whole way. She hit a button on her laptop and it came to life. After a few minutes she tapped a few keys and Facebook popped up. She started scrolling through females faces and names.

"These are all ya friends. They state and worldwide since you've been out and we started this for you. you've racked up 847 friends and a lot of em want you to come to their city and state," she said.

"Damn!" was all I could say.

"On toppa all that you've still got a lotta friend requests on here too." She showed me. It said I had over 30 requests and I really didn't know what to say. "Your Instagram jumpin too," and she showed me that page as well. D showed me the videos that were posted by women from the parties and the hundreds of the comments that were posted, too.

"Damn, a nigga didn't think this would jump so hard, so soon," I told Kim.

"Yeah nigga. You welcome," she said with a playful attitude.

"Thank you ma," I said, giving her a small peck on the lips. I looked at the time and it was getting close to 2 PM. I had to go meet the guys in a few, but I still had a lil time to spare.

"Oh, and before I head out, a woman I did a show for. Well, I found out she writes stories for some magazine, but I ran the idea by her and she thought I had something good. But we're short the manpower right now, so she thought we could continue letting women take the photos with fellas and post them on those pages and leave our info with it. But what I was thinking next was to get some t-shirts made," I told her, giving her time to consider everything.

"That's wassup. I'll work on the t-shirts thing and keep this shit jumpin. But in the meantime, I got an itch that needs to be scratched," she said, grabbing a handful of my dick and balls and squeezing.

"Mmm...I got you ma, but I gotta go meet the fellas, so rain check that for me and I'll make it worth the wait," I told her. She gave it some thought, gave my dick one last squeeze, and released me.

"I'll get back at you lata," I told her, and headed out so I could go meet the fellas at the gym.

—•—

When I pulled up to Planet Fitness I noticed a familiar car parked beside Raheem's box Chevy. Then I remembered, that was BG's ride. I motioned for him to get out and follow me into the gym.

"Wassup bro? It's good you showed up. My homegirl must told you we'd be here?" I asked him.

"Yeah, she did. I really need a job E," he said.

"Fam, I'ma tell you now that we getting money, but we putting it toward building an empire, and once we open the club then shit will get better," I told him.

"That's straight. I got faith in you bro," BG said.

"Bet. Well let's go get this money." We headed inside and I introduce him to my team of guys and my right-hand Gee.

—•—

When we got done hitting that steel and chopping it up, it was a little after 5 PM. I figured it was time to shut it down. "That's good fellas! I ain't tryna burn ya'll out before we turn up for the weekend. Let's go get a bite to eat," I told everybody.

We grabbed our things and headed to this nice fish spot up the street. Gee jumped in his Denali, Sam and Stephon rode with Raheem, because they was all from the Bluff, AB just moved to Arkansas in Monticello, so he drove this black on chrome Crown Vic. BG trailed us in his old school Delta 88 with a quarter rag top. It was decked out, but I knew once the fellas started making money they'd upgrade.

The fish spot we headed to is where I met a few women when I first stepped out the joint, and this bad lil chocolate female that calls herself T-Baby worked there, so I know she'd give a nigga a discount.

We pulled in and parked side by side, then headed toward the entrance. "I hope you niggas brought an appetite," I told them, and we busted out laughing. As we filed into the restaurant I saw that T-Baby was at the counter.

"What's up E?" she asked, looking excited to see me.

"What's good ma? I need a table for seven, and we'll have that big fish platter with extra coleslaw, fries, hush puppies, extra bread. Is that okay with you fellas?" I turned and asked. Everyone nodded in agreement.

"Damn, these some big ass dudes," she said, and some other females came from the back to scope out my team.

"Yeah, and I gotta feed dese negros," I said, and we laughed on our way to the table.

"Oh, and can I get 7 sweet teas?" I asked T as we pushed two tables together.

"I gotchu, E. I'll be right back," she said, and headed toward the kitchen. Bob's famous fish has changed since the last time I seen it.

As we waited on our food and drinks, a few females came out and began talking to a couple of the guys.

"What do ya'll do that requires you to be so big?" this skinny, light skinned female with braces asked.

"We're male strippers ma," Raheem answered, because she stood closest to him.

"Why come we haven't heard of ya'll?" she asked.

"I guess ya'll just don't get out like that," he replied.

"Nah, I don't. But do ya'll have some shows ya'll done?"

"Yeah. Here check this out," I jumped in, handing her my phone. She looked at the videos that were on Instagram. The fellas didn't know that they'd been videoed when doing their shows.

"Damnnnn! Ya'll be doing ya'll thing!" a dark-skinned female said, standing behind braces and looking over her shoulder. "So who are you?" she asked, singling me out.

"I'm the CEO of this empire, and these guys you looking at, they're the A-team," I told the girls.

"Do ya'll got, like, stage names or sum?" she asked, and the fellas began introducing themselves.

"They call me Gee," Gee said.

"I'm Payday," Sam said.

"What bout ya'll two?" her friend asked.

"I'm Cool Off," Stephon said.

"Why is that?" Braces asked with a flirty smile.

"Because when it's time for ya to cool off, call me," he replied, and they giggled.

"They call me Young Hardbody," Raheem spoke up, and just stood up and lifted up his shirt. Braces ran her hands on his abs.

"Damnnnn!" she said.

"Aye! Ya'll get ya'lls hot asses to work and stop bothering my customers!" some old school brotha yelled from behind the counter as T-Baby was bringing a pitcher of iced tea and cups out.

"Here ya'll go E," she said, and right behind her Braces came out with a couple girls carrying platters of fish, fries, hush puppies, and one had a bowl of coleslaw and plate of bread.

"Finally! A nigga starving afta that workout," Stephon said. He was the smallest of the bunch but could eat his ass off. We blessed the meal and began to eat like we were all a big ass family.

"So, how can we see ya'll?" Braces asked.

"Here's a card, and T-Baby knows how to get in touch with us," I said in between bites of my fish sandwich.

"Okay, bet. Ya'll enjoy the food and hopefully we get a chance to see ya'lls show," she said and her and the females that came with her walked off. T-Baby gave me a nod and said she'd let us eat and she's talk to me later.

"Oh — and what I want to talk to you fellas about is the women we've conquered just from the little shows we've done round the town," I said. "We've got em ranging from the east coast to the west. Midwest to the south, and we even got them overseas saying they'd pay to come see us. But I'm starting a magazine up, and it's gonna be called Hard Bodies. Think about this: ya'll did two shows each and made over $1,200, so imagine what ya'll make traveling and with magazine sales."

I stopped and gave them time to let this sink in and finished my sandwich.

"I'm with you Big E," Raheem spoke up and everybody nodded together.

"I preciate ya'll having my back. We keep working hard and I promise it'll pay off. I'm working on getting more talent. That way we can travel and ya'll can take a break. I already paid for the meal, I got somewhere to be, ya'll take it easy and be safe," I said, giving all the fellas dap and standing. "Oh — and when the magazine gets started, ya'll be ready to tell about yourselves," I added, and headed out.

—•—

The afternoon heat rushed me upon leaving Bob's Fish Spot. I was already in my car on the road when it slipped my mind to tell Gee that he and BG would be partners. I texted it to him and he replied *Ok*.

After a few minutes I sent him another message about meeting at the gym Saturday at the same time. I cranked up that "No Days Off" by Fetty Wap and grabbed my phone to check on Sunni and see if she needed anything on my way home.

"Hey bae, where you at?" she answered, sounding tired.

"I'm on my way home now. Why what's wrong ma?" I asked.

"Nothing's wrong, I was just wondering when you coming back is all."

"Oh, I'm coming now. What you doing anyway?" I asked her.

"Nothing. My sister Nikki showed up and brought me something to eat and can't wait to meet you."

"Alright well I'm almost to the house, I'll talk to ya'll when I get home."

"Okay bae, drive safe," she said and we disconnected the call. I turned my music back up and put a blunt in me before I got home, and my thoughts drifted to everything I've got accomplished while bumpin "Run tha Streetz" by Tupac.

I hit my street and saw a silver Nissan Maxima with some nice rims and tinted windows. I took that to be Sunni's sister's car. I parked on the street so I wouldn't block her in and chewed on a piece of cinnamon gum. Followed that up with a spray of Polo Red, trying to drown out the smell of that pressure.

When I made it in the house I could smell what smelled like Chinese food, so me having the munchies, I headed straight for the kitchen and seen the containers of food on the middle bar. I made me a plate of fried rice, noodles, egg rolls and Teriyaki wings.

"Bae is that you!?" Sunni yelled from the bedroom.

"Yeah!" I yelled back and heard footsteps and low giggling coming down the way.

"Hey bae! Why didn't you come see me before you decided to come in here and smash our Chinese food?" Sunni asked playfully.

"I was hungry girl and I'm tired," I responded.

"Damn, hungry ass nigga! Sunni you didn't tell me your baby daddy is a baby gorilla!" Nikki said and we all laughed.

"How you doing Nik, my name's Evan but everybody calls me Big E," I said.

"It's good to meet you E. I'm the big sista Nicole, but everyone calls me Nikki," she introduced herself, sitting on the other bar stool. "So what kind of work you do?" she asked.

"My baby's a stripper!" Sunni told her.

"For real! Where you work at?" Nikki asked.

"We do house calls right now, but I'm going to open me a building up soon, then you'll see what it's really about."

"Alright, that's wassup."

"I'm working on getting me a magazine started too. It's gonna be called Hard Bodies Magazine, but I'm still working the kinks out," I told her, finishing my plate. Sunni put it in the dish washer and came to stand by me as I was talking to her sister.

"So you think dis gonna jump?" Nikki asked.

"Yeah, I got faith in it, and besides, I got a lotta females lined up on the books and videos posted on Instagram," I told her.

"I'ma have to check that out," she said.

"Me too," Sunni chimed in.

"Bae, I was gonna show you but it slipped my mind — here's

the pages here," I said, grabbing her tablet that was at my end of the bar and logging into Facebook and Instagram so they could check it out.

"Damnit bae, this is hot! My brotha needs a job too. He been down bad," Sunni said, scrolling through photos and videos.

"Tell him to call me and we'll see what's up. But I got some calls to make, I'ma holla at ya'll in a minute," I told the women, grabbing my phone and heading to our room. I scrolled through my contacts and called Red again, and this time he answered, "Hello?"

"What's good with you Red?" I asked.

"Who is dis?" he shot back.

"Man this Big E. Evan Barrow."

"Aww shit bro, wassup! It's been a minute since I've heard from you. How you doing?" he asked.

"I'm alright man just tryna get myself together. What you been out there doing?"

"Not shit, the same old stuff when you was out here, just got into the trappin business too."

"Shit bro, you want a good job making good money?" I asked him.

"Yeah, but what you got jumping first?"

"I got a male stripper service going and it's good money too. Bruh I really need the help."

"Yeah, I might take you up on that, but aye, I got some shit jumping and I'ma have to hit you back," Red said.

"Alright, keep in touch and I'll get you down here and we can catch up," I told him.

"Alright," he said, and we disconnected. I headed back to the kitchen to check on the women.

"Did ya'll get a hold of ya'lls brother?" I asked, coming into the kitchen and the women were still in the same spot.

"Nah, but we left a message though," Nikki said, trying to kiss Sunni and she pulled her head back.

"What's wrong witchu?" I asked her.

"Looks like you were really into ya job!" she replied with an attitude.

"Ma, slow ya roll. That's all it is — a job! I don't know none of dem women and now that I've found someone to replace me, I'm running this business from home," I replied.

"Good, cause I don't want dem hoes hands on you or your dick!" she snapped.

"Well that's my cue. I'ma holla at ya sis. You take care, E," Nikki said, hugging us before leaving.

"I'ma get me a shower bae and get some sleep when I get out," I said, heading to our room.

—•—

After a quick 20 minute shower, I walked out the bathroom with a towel round my waist and stopped in my tracks. Sunni had her legs gaped open rubbing on her swollen pussy.

"Damn, what took you so long?" she asked.

"Umm —" I was speechless and rock hard instantly. I dropped the towel and climbed on the bed ready to dick her down. I kissed her manicured toes and kissed my way up her thighs until I came to her sweet center. I placed a soft kiss on her pussy and sucked her soft clit in my mouth.

"Ssss...eat dat pussy daddy!" she cried out and eat that pussy I did.

After finger fucking her and sucking on that clit, I felt her body begin to shake. "I'm cumming baby!" she called out, and her body and legs began to shake harder. I rose up and licked her sweet juices off my lips and let her lil nerves calm down.

She rose up on her elbows as I began to crawl up the bed, dick rubbing up her thigh. As I began to slide my dick in, I must've gave off a look of concern for the baby because she said, "Bae, the baby is gonna be fine, now gimme that D!"

She groaned, grabbing my rock hardness and guiding me in her. I gave her that D for a few hours.

———•———

After I came long and hard in that pussy, I collapsed beside her and she rolled over on my chest and kissed me.

"I hope your sister don't tell ya folks about the baby," I said.

"Nah, I told her not to, because I was gonna tell em in due time," she replied.

"Aight. Bet. Let me get a quick shower and get dressed, I got some business to handle bae."

"Okay, be safe out there E," she told me while I was heading to the shower.

When I came out the shower Sunni was out cold. I looked at the clock on the nightstand and it was only 8:43 PM. I grabbed me a pair of boxers and Polo socks, then headed to the closet, grabbed a pair of my 501 jeans, a v-neck and pair of Airmax and got dressed real quick before going into the safe and grabbing a lil over five bands.

Sunni didn't know, but I was bout to make her an honest woman. As I walked out the house I called ahead to Kay's Jeweler and asked would they give me a chance to make it to em. I told the woman on the phone what I was looking for and she said she'd wait. So I jumped in my BMW and hit that highway in a rush.

———•———

I pulled into the jewelry store parking lot around 9:15 and it was a gold Lexus in front, so I figured that was the woman I spoke to. I parked beside it and went to the door. It was locked, so I tapped on the glass and a minute or so later a slim white woman with platinum blonde hair came to the door.

"Are you the guy I spoke with about an engagement ring?" she asked behind the door.

"Yes ma'am." And with that said she let me in and quickly locked the door again.

"Right this way please," she said, directing me to a glass display case. "Here are some of the newest rings we've got on display that just came in Mr...?"

"Oh, I'm sorry for the rudeness. My name's Evan," I told her, extending my hand over the counter.

"I'm Lori, the store manager, but as I was saying, these are the newest rings, kinda pricey, but guaranteed the woman you're proposing to will be more than happy," she said and I took my time looking through some of the gold engagement rings.

I chose gold because it matches Sunni's skin tone and she has this gold necklace she always wears.

"She wears a size 8, I like this gold carat in a half triple row with diamonds," I said, reading off the label.

"That's a good choice sir."

"You can call me Evan ma," I told her.

"Sorry Evan. That's an amazing ring," she finished.

"Okay, well I want that one then and I want it in the all-white case with gold lining," I told her.

"Evan, did you look at the price tag?" she asked. I chuckled lightly and reached deep in my pocket for the bank roll I had grabbed out the safe.

"Lori, does it look like I'm hurting for money, or wanna be cheap? I treat my women not beat them," I told her. Her eyes were locked on the fist-full of blue gods I had in my hand.

"Sorry sir — I mean Evan. I'll ring that up for you and I'll throw in a year of jewelry cleaning for you too," she told me and went to the back with the ring I picked out. She returned a couple minutes later with a small black bag.

"That'll be $4,018.05," she said. I counted out $4,020 and passed it to her.

"Thank you," I said not waiting on a receipt, and heading for the door. I heard the locks slide open and I walked out into the cool night air.

I looked at my phone and it was almost 10. I headed for the Shell on University to gas up and grab me a sprite before going home.

Sunni

I woke up to someone banging on the front door. I looked at the nightstand clock and it was after 10 PM. E was still out. I grabbed my .380 out the nightstand and headed to the door.

"Who the fuck is it?" I said, approaching the door.

"Nigga this ya brotha, open the door!" Lance yelled through it.

"Bro do you know what time it is?" I asked, swinging it open. Lance was a burly ass Negro. He was about 6'5" and 260lbs, but he was all muscle. He was my skin complexion and my dad's build. He was my dad's junior alright and that's why our mom named him a junior.

"Hey baby sista! What's been up witchu?" he asked with that deep voice sounding like a light skin Vin Diesel.

"Not shit bro, just tryna get myself together, but come in and make yourself at home," I told him and he had to duck down to come through the door.

"I heard you got yourself a man now," he said.

"Yeah. His name is Evan and he should be back in a minute," I told him.

"Is this the nigga you said got a job for me?" he asked.

"Yes Lance, so hear him out before you say anything," I told him and that's when I seen headlights in the window and heard music bumping. I knew my man was home.

"I'll be right back!" I said, leaving Lance in the living room.

Big E

When I pulled up at my house it was after 10 PM and it was a black Navigator on some 28-inch Asanti's. I've never seen this truck before, but I was about to meet the owner. Before I got out I took the ring out the bag and stuffed it in my pocket and stepped out. I was met at the door by Sunni and some big light skin nigga standing behind her.

She had her .380 in her hand so that instantly put me on the defense with this nigga. She threw her arms around my neck and kissed me. I kissed her back, but my eyes never left this nigga. I grabbed the gun from her.

"Bae you okay?" I asked, keeping my voice low and eyeing this nigga.

"Yeah I'm cool, but bae…"

"Bro, can I ask what you doing at my house this time of night?" I interrupted, approaching him with the .380 ready to sit this nigga out if he said the wrong thing.

"Woah now big fella! I come to see my baby sister and see this nigga I'm figuring is you bout a job. But don't get the skin tone and boyish looks confused, I'm wit da shit now," he said, raising his shirt and showing me an all chrome Beretta with a pearl handle.

"Awww…okay my bad my nigga. Can't be too careful round here. They call me E, bruh," I said, extending my hand.

"Lance my guy, and it's good to see my sister's got a nigga that's protective," he said shaking my hand.

"Bae if you woulda given me the chance to introduce ya'll you can see that this my brother!" Sunni yelled at me.

"I'm sorry bae, I reacted before I could think, it won't happen again." I told her, giving her the gun to put up and we headed to the living room to talk.

"So what kinda business you run bruh-law?" Lance asked sitting on the loveseat and flipping through the TV.

"Man I'ma keep it real — I'ma open a male strip club in Lil Rock," I told him. He looked at me and busted out laughing. Then he looked at me again and seen the serious look on my face.

"Aww shit, you serious ain'tcha?" he asked.

"Yeah, I already got some dudes behind me now but I can always use the help."

"Well fam, I'ma tell you I ain't doing no stripping, but if you need security or sum I'm the man fa tha job, but I ain't doing no strippin through," he repeated.

"That's cool too bruh. Is the pistol registered?" I asked.

"Hell yeah, can't be too safe out here in the line of work I do," he replied.

"What kinda work you do anyways if you don't mind me asking?" I asked.

"Let's just say I buy, sell, and trade goods," he told me with a smirk. Then I noticed that he was draped in jewelry. A nice rose gold Jesus piece, Rolex, and pinky ring to match.

"Well I can use your help, just don't mix your work on the job. I don't wanna build this empire and it falls because of a slip up," I told him with a look of concern on my face.

"Big bruh, I got you, just call me when you need me. Sunni has my number," he said, rising to his feet. He was taller than me by a few inches and outweighed me by about 10 lbs., but that's what I needed at my front door.

"It's always good to have some more help behind me," I replied.

"I gotchu bro, just holla at me but I'm bout to be out, get at me," Lance said, walking out the door. I sat there looking at the late-night show before I got up to make my way to the room. Sunni was on her side snoring lightly. I kicked off my Airmax's and went to the dresser and got a pair of gym shorts to change into. Once I changed I hid the ring, deciding to wait for the right moment. I curled up next to Sunni and dozed off myself.

—•—

The next morning I was woken up to the doorbell ringing. Sunni was still passed out. I rolled from under her and got up to answer the door. When I snatched the door open Babygirl jumped into my arms.

"Morning Daddy!" she said excitedly. I pulled her into the house and Mama G came in behind her and closed the door.

I put Babygirl down and gave Mama G a hug too.

"So how'd it go?" I asked.

"We went to the movies and Mama G showed me some more of her recipes," Babygirl squealed.

"Yeah, I showed her the secret to my finga lickin greens and my hot water corn bread," Mama G said.

"Well a brother sho' can't wait to taste ya cooking," I told her.

"Every time Sunni cooks, you getting a taste," she replied.

"Yeah you right," I said and we busted out laughing.

"Where's Sunni at anyways?" Mama G asked, taking a seat on the full sized couch.

"Aw, she still laying down. You want me to go get her up?" I asked.

"Yeah, if you don't mind."

I went to get Sunni for her mom and when I walked in the room she was coming out the bathroom. "Bae, ya ma wants you," I told her as she finished putting her hair up in a pony-tail. I went back into the living room with Sunni on my heels.

"Hey mama," Sunni said, still sounding tired.

"Hey baby, how you been?" Mama G asked.

"I'm good, been helping E get his business plans together for his club, and now I gotta get a liquor license," Sunni replied.

"Aww. Okay. You talking bout for that male stripper service? I might swing by and check it out!" Mama G said.

"Cool," I replied with a laugh.

"But E we having Sunday dinner next week and would love for you to join us?" she asked.

"Okay, me and Sunni will be over after church around 1:30."

"That's a perfect time." I looked over at Babygirl, who was playing on her phone.

"Well I better get back home to this grouchy man. Babygirl come give Gramma G a hug and I'll see you soon," she said, giving Babygirl a hug, then Sunni a hug too before leaving.

She still didn't know Sunni was pregnant, and Sunni didn't know I was gonna propose Sunday. I looked at the living room clock and it was a little past noon. I figured I'd take Babygirl out with me and let Sunni get some rest.

I headed to the bedroom where Sunni was back in bed flipping through the TV and Babygirl was laying beside her. I got dressed in a pair of Nike shorts, a t-shirt, and my Airmax. I sprayed a little bit of my Polo Red on, brushed my grill, washed my face, and I was ready to go. I walked out the bathroom and they were still in the same spot.

"Babygirl you wanna ride with me to your Aunt Kay's?" I asked.

"Yeah! I miss Aunt Kay," she said excitedly. She jumped off the bed and went to get ready.

"Bae, you need anything before I leave?" I asked Sunni.

"Nah, I'm just tired. But give Kay my love," she replied, snuggling under the fluffy comforter.

I grabbed the keys to her Q50 and met Babygirl at the living room door. We headed out, I locked the door behind us, and Babygirl rushed to the passenger side as I unlocked the car.

We settled in and I let her know I'd stop and get her something to eat on the way to Kay's. She just nodded and buckled up, playing with the radio. I just smiled, thinking, *My baby is mature for a 9-year-old.* I bagged out and headed toward Little Rock, bobbing my head to a Cardi B song on Power 92.

Pulling up at Kay's, Babygirl wrapped up the rest of her Subway sandwich and was ready to jump out before I could put the car in park. I knew she was ready to see her aunt, it had been a week or so that they'd been apart, and from the looks of it she had a few friends over waiting for her to show up.

I parked on the street and we hopped out. Before we could even knock the door came open and Kay was waiting for us.

"Damn! Finally! I was starting to think I wasn't going to see my Babygirl or brother again," Kay said with a big smile on her face.

"Nah I just been a little busy but what's good with you?" I asked, hugging my sister. She stepped to the side to let us out of the heat and into some A/C.

"Not too much, just been tryna maintain and find my bro some business."

"For real? That's wassup, thank you," I told her.

"You all did such a good job that the girls up the street been talking, and there's definitely some interest around here for that kind of thing. You came up with a good plan E. I'm starting to see how it's all going to come together."

It felt good to have my sister behind me, not that she ever doubted me, but now she was seeing the success I had planned.

We walked through the living room to where her friends were sitting in the den, talking amongst themselves and listening to music. Babygirl sat beside this pretty yellow bone and she began playing with Babygirl's hair, so I figured this woman and my daughter were familiar with each other. Especially the way they were laughing and carrying on.

"Sis but can I holla atcha for a sec?" I asked Kay with a head nod. We went into the back bedroom.

"Wassup bro?" she asked, looking concerned.

"Aye, umm...Babygirl's gonna be living with me and Sunni from now on," I told her.

"Evan, you're saying this like I won't never get a chance to see her again. That's yo baby, I just help you raise her while you get yourself straight," she replied with a grin.

"I appreciate it too, thank you sis, but let me know wassup wit ya homegirls. I still got some money I need to save up."

"Alright bet," she agreed.

As we headed back to the living room I heard them in there laughing and cheering. Once we walked in I saw Babygirl showing off her dance moves. I just sat back and laughed as well. When she finally made eye contact, I waved her over to me.

"Go ahead and pack your stuff and what you can't get, we'll get later," I told her, and she jetted off to the bedroom. My phone began to vibrate in my pocket. The caller ID told me it was Gee.

"Wassup bro?"

"Not shit, had some stuff running through my head and needed to holla atcha," he replied.

"I'm kinda busy right now, but just run it by me at the gym Sunday," I told him.

"Alright, that's cool too. I'ma scream atcha Sunday then."

"Cool, and ya'll hold it down too and look out for BG too, try to keep that nigga busy," I told him before we agreed and hung up. Babygirl came in the living room dragging two duffels full of clothes.

"Dang! You bagged the whole room didn't you?" I asked and she punched me in the side.

"Nope, just all my clothes. That's it," she replied laughing.

"Alright well go give ya Aunt Kay a hug before we take off. We'll come back another time to pick up the rest of your stuff."

She ran in the living room as I carried her bags to the car.

"You just make sho' you come back and spend the night with Auntie," Kay said to Babygirl as she followed her to the car. I gave her a hug and jumped in the driver's seat of Sunni's Q50.

Kay headed back in the house because it was hot as hell and it was only 2 o'clock. I waited on Babygirl to get buckled in before I pulled off, and we headed home.

As we drove I got to thinking bout my plans, daughter, and the new baby we bout to bring into this world. But when I got this club jumping and my magazine started, I wouldn't have to worry bout nothing. It was all coming together.

—•—

When I pulled up beside my BMW I noticed some lil girls outside next door. One of the girls who looked like she was mixed with something walked up to Babygirl once we parked and asked could she come over for a while.

"When she gets done unpacking she can, unless ya'll help her, and she'll get done faster," I told em and they volunteered, so I carried the bags in the house for them and to the room which was now hers, and left the girls to they work.

Sunni was in the kitchen whipping up something that smelled good as hell.

"What you making ma?" I asked.

"Some fried chicken, mashed potatoes with gravy, and some mac n' cheese," she said, singing along to the Monica song she had on the radio.

"Yeah, a brotha sure is hungry," I told her, kissing her on the cheek before taking a seat at the table.

"I got a lil show to do for some women at Kay's, I won't be gone long. I just wanted to get Babygirl back to da house and out this heat. Can you believe it's 101 outside?" I asked her.

"Yeah, I can believe it. I went to check the mailbox and damn near fell out it was so hot!" she said laughing.

"Bae, you need to stay off ya feet too," I told her with a concerned look on my face.

"Babe I go this! You just make sure you keep bringing dat bread home for momma and the baby," she replied with some cockiness in her voice.

"You just make sho you feed my baby and put me a big ass plate up so I can shower and eat when I come home," I told her, leaning back in my chair and crossing my arms over my barrel chest.

Babygirl and her friends were done with unpacking, and she hugged me and Sunni before running out the house.

"Well I'ma go ahead and get back over there before it gets too late and shit, because I wanna spend the rest of my night with you," I told Sunni before getting up and heading back to Kay's. It was turning 3 PM so I knew I'd be home before 10, because I wanted to lay down with bae tonight.

I got outside and it was humid as hell, so I hurried and jump in my BMW and let the windows down and the sunroof back. I turned the radio on Power 92, rolled me a blunt real quick, and hit the highway.

—•—

Pulling back up at Kay's, it was a couple more cars added to what I seen a little while ago, so I had to park on the street. I got out, eyes low to the earth and really feeling freaky.

I observed my hood and noticed ain't much changed in John Barrow, but they fixed up a few houses. I wanted something to drink so I hurried in the house where I heard the music coming from. You could smell that pressure in the air and hear the women giggling in the living room.

When I made it to the room Kay was the first one to spot me.

"Brotha, I thought you wasn't coming back!" she said, and I could tell she was damn near ready to tip over.

"Nah, I gotta make this money, my guys are doing they thang so I had to come get it over with," I told her.

"Cool, come have a drank with me," she said, pulling me toward her mini bar in the living room. I made me a gin and OJ and downed that real quick. Then I looked for Kay, who had wandered off.

She was back in her spot on the couch talking to some mixed chikas. I went and grabbed her and told her, "Come dance with ya brotha!" tryna get the party started.

When the women seen me and Kay dancing around goofing off, they joined the fun. The mixed chick jumped up and eyed me before grabbing me from my sister and threw that tight lil ass on my dick.

She got to popping that ass, rubbing it up and down my dick and I couldn't help but get hard, I'm a man! That pressure was in me and that drank was taking over.

I grabbed lil mama by the hips and threw that dick back on her. We got more cheers even from Kay.

"Nigga you say you a strippa, then strip nigga!" some black ass female said. She had a big gap in her teeth and favored Precious in the face, but the bitch had a banging body. Normally that wouldn't be my type of toast because I couldn't put no butter on that shit, but tonight was different, so I got into my real "freak" mode.

I pulled my shirt off and that's when the money got to flying. My sister don't fuck with no broke bitches, so I knew I had to get these hoes turnt up. I snatched my shorts off and they went crazy. Mixed chick had a tattoo on her lower back that said "Vanessa," so I figured that was her name.

"Damn! Girl do you see dat shit!" the black female turned around and I lifted Vanessa up and threw her on the floor, her eyes got big.

She reached up and began rubbing my semi hard dick. I began grinding all between her legs and she dry humped me back. I slid all the way up her face and ground that dick all in her face before sliding down again and grinding her pussy through the floor.

"Damn Nessa you might as well fuck the nigga!" Blacky said and they all laughed and she turned red in the face.

I helped her up and they got to cheering and shit. I looked at the black ass female and approached her shit talking ass with a mean look on my face.

"Nah nigga I'm married!" was the protest that spilled from her lips. I got near her and she fell back on the couch, looking up at me. She was a short female too, so I jumped up on the couch, feet on each side of her and threw that dick in her face too.

"Yeahhh! He got ya ass now Tasha! Talk that shit now!" Nessa yelled as the women turned up and I seen money began to run on the couch.

"Ssss!" was all that came out of her lips. I felt her mouth open and she bit down on my dick lightly and let go. Now that had me turned the fuck up. I knew if I didn't get off her, my dick was gonna be in her mouth forreal.

"Ohhh! Girl! She bite that mu'fucka!" some red bone with microbraids said.

"Nah E! Get your big ass off my couch!" Kay said, coming back into the living room. I ground her face a few more times before climbing down.

I danced with a few more chicks before I realized it was getting late. I got dressed and collected all my money up and hugged everybody before telling Kay I had to ride. It was almost 8 PM then.

I hit the door and it had started to cool down, and had a slight breeze too. I was sweating too so that breeze felt good. I jumped in my ride and hit the other half of my blunt and was getting ready to pull off.

"Get down E!" I heard a female yell, and I looked up to see Tasha coming outside.

"Wassup ma?" I asked, finishing off my half a blunt and texting Sunni, letting her know I was on my way.

"Can you run me to the store real quick?" she asked and as she got closer I noticed that this chocolate mu'fucka was thicker than I thought. She had on some daisy dukes, pink and white shoes, and a pink and white shirt that hugged her titties and said "Pink" across the front and them lips was supa fat and glossed up.

"Yeah I gotchu. Hop in I gotta get home."

I unlocked the door and let her in. I laid my seat back, turned up that "Pass Out" by Quevo as I pulled off.

I looked over and Tasha's skin complexion gave her a sex appeal, and them lips, hips and ass added to it. She had light brown eyes to be so black and that made her even more appealing. I guess I had to look at her good, because she looked good in my passenger seat.

Tasha

After that nigga put that monster in my face and I bit it and felt it throb in my mouth, I knew I had to satisfy my thirst. My pussy was wet and this nigga was gonna fuck me and let me swallow dat dick before he head home.

I ran to the bathroom, freshened up, and threw some gloss on my luscious ass lips. Coming out the bathroom I heard E telling everybody he was leaving. The ladies were all huddled up and sitting around like school girls talking.

"Girl I'll be right back. I gotta get some squares," I told Kay and before I walked out, she just told me to be careful with a wink and devilish grin.

I headed out and caught him just in time. I asked him to run me to the store and he eye balled me up and down before agreeing. I climbed in the passenger seat of his fly ass red BMW with the leather seats warm against my ass.

I knew from the way he looked at me I was gonna get a quick fix before he got home.

Big E

We pulled up at the hood corner store.

"Nah, pull around back," Tasha said, laying her hands on my semi hard dick, and I knew what was up then.

I rolled up the windows and pulled around back where a small alley was, and it was dark. She began pulling off her shorts and I pulled out my dick and stroked it to life.

"Here, let me do that for you," she said, and grabbed my dick and began stroking me to complete hardness.

I looked like a monster in her tiny, soft, manicured hands. I slid my seat all the way back and she leaned over and placed kisses around the tip before swallowing me whole. She deep throated me for a minute before she was ready for the dick. She climbed in the seat and put her ass up in the air. I hit the side button and slid her seat back and climbed behind her, ready to punish the pussy.

She was tight upon entry but once we got going I knew it was a matter of time before I busted and slid in her raw. She began throwing that ass back and I had to brace myself using the dashboard.

"Fuuuuck dis pussy baby!" she cried out. I gripped those wide ass hips and buried the dick deep into her as far as I could. "Arrrgh! Fuck this pussy daddy!" she screamed and began to throw that ass back even harder. I felt that pussy start to contract and knew she was getting her nut.

"Ughhh! I'm cumming baby!" she screamed and right at that time the walls began to squeeze around my dick, and I felt my nut coming.

"I'm bouta cum ma!" I growled. She pushed me back against the dashboard and slammed my dick down her throat. She sucked all the vitamins and nutrients from me.

After my dick went limp in her mouth, she cleaned me up

with a few more licks and I rolled back into the driver's seat and pulled my shorts back up.

"Here you go boo," she said, handing me two hunnid dollar bills.

"Bet," I told her.

"If you throw that dick like that again, I'ma break you off again," she said.

"Nah ma, that's just a one-time thing. But ya shit is fiya though!" I responded, starting the car after she got dressed. I pulled back around to the front, and she got out to go get what she was wanting.

———•———

When we pulled up back at Kay's house it looked like they were still kicking it and Kay and some friends were on the porch smoking a blunt. When Kay saw me pull up, she came down the stairs toward my ride as her friend got out and headed back toward the house. They exchanged words, laughed, and Kay continued toward me. I rolled the window down as she approached.

"You alright brotha?" she asked, and I could smell the liquor on her breath.

"Yeah, I'm good, but I'll be back sometime tomorrow to talk some B.I. with you, and I gotta go to Lil Jon's spot to get his shit and need ya help. Do you know where he live at?" I asked.

"Nah, he moved around a lot after his business picked up. But text me the address and I'll meet you over there," Kay replied.

"Bet, well here go a lil something for ya pocket," and I gave her the two hundred I just got from her friend.

"'Preciate it bro, I'ma holla atcha later," Kay said, sticking the bills in her bra and heading back to her friends. I rolled my window back up to block out the afternoon heat and headed home thinking of this meal I was bout to put in my stomach. I texted Sunni before I pulled off, asking her do she need anything.

She wanted ice cream and cookies like always.

I gotchu, I replied, turned my music up and hit the highway and headed toward Walmart before going home.

——•——

When I pulled up at the house, the neighborhood was quiet, but the sun was still tearing down the street.

You had some kids out having water balloon fights and having fun. I parked behind Sunni's Q50 and with the ice cream and cookies in hand, rushed toward the front door.

It was 102 out today. I felt my phone vibrate and knew it was just a text. I made it in the house, breaking a sweat. Hell, just standing outside you'd break a sweat.

"Bae where you at?" I yelled out for Sunni.

"I'm in the living room," she yelled back. I kicked off my shoes at the door, went and grabbed my plate out the microwave and put bae's ice cream and cookies up, because I knew she wanted to wait until I ate so we could share.

Walking into the living room, Sunni was propped up in her favorite spot watching Proud Mary. "Did you just start it?" I asked.

"Yup," she said, and I sat beside her, plate on the coffee table, and began to demolish my food.

"What took you so long?" she asked. I looked at the clock and it was after 8 PM.

"Ran into my homeboy Rudy and we just lost track of time, but you know I'm always in the recruitment class, so

I gave him a rundown of the business and he was interested. Gave him a card, now I'm here with you," I replied.

"Oh okay. Well eat your food so we can eat some ice cream," Sunni said, rushing me to finish. As soon as I did she went to get the ice cream and two spoons.

"Text Babygirl for me and tell her to come home for a minute," I told her as she came back in the living room. She flopped down and grabbed her phone, punched a few buttons, and about five minutes later Babygirl came through the front door.

"You wanted me daddy?" Babygirl asked.

"Yeah, I need to talk to ya for a minute," I replied. She came and sat beside me on the couch. "Alright, check this out. For one, I don't need you at some folks house like that." She just nodded but listened. "And two, you talking bout money. You need to complete ya chores around the house and I'll make sure you got something in your pocket every Friday. Save ya money and don't be quick to spend it in one place," I told her.

"Okay daddy," she said and leaned back into the couch and glanced at the TV.

"Have you eaten?" I asked Babygirl.

"Yeah, I came home earlier and ate," she said. I handed her my spoon and told Sunni I'm bout to grab me a shower and left the girls watching TV.

After stepping under the shower head and letting the hot water wash the stress off, I heard banging on the door.

"Daddy! Ya phone ringing!" Babygirl was yelling.

"Aight! Tell Sunni to answer it!" I yelled back. I soaped up and rinsed off a couple times, shaved my head, and stepped out the shower. I got myself together and emerged from the bathroom feeling refreshed.

Sunni was still watching TV when I stepped in the living room.

"Ms. D called bae. She said call her when you got the chance," Sunni said, handing me my phone. She never got in my business when it came to trying to start this club up. She never questioned my money, she just made sure everything was straight.

"I'll be right back," I told her, kissing her and going to the bedroom. I never talked business in front of Babygirl or Sunni.

I checked my texts and I had a few which were from some potential customers, and one from Tasha. I deleted that one but I did save her number and sent her a quick reply.

Know where we stand. I've got a family to support!

After I sent the message I deleted it and called Ms. D.

"Where ya bald headed ass been!" she snapped, answering on the first ring.

"Damn, I didn't know I had a parole officer!" I snapped back.

"Don't get smart nigga! But anyways, some lady named Shonequa called and said for you to call her. And your friend Red said he want to go into business witchu," Ms. D said.

Red was going to bring me all my female customers up in Chicago, so I had to get back at him ASAP.

"Aight. Bet. Have you found some more shows for the fellas yet?" I asked.

"Yeah, I already got that squared away, and I sent them letters off. I should hear back soon," she told me.

"Cool, I'ma get back atcha in the morning. I'ma swing by and we not gonna be using Facebook much longer for our business. Let me call this lady. I'll get back atcha later," I told her and disconnected the call.

I went through my contacts and found Shonequa's number and gave her a call. My phone said it was after 9 PM. I really needed to get me some sleep, because I had a long day ahead of me tomorrow.

"Wassup Evan!" Shonequa said, sounding excited and addressing me by my first name.

"Wassup maa? Whatchu got going?" I asked.

"Nothin much, just tryna get everything together for your magazine," she replied.

"What all'd you get done so far?" I asked with curiosity.

"I talked to my guy in Cali and I've gotta get ya'lls story lines, and some photos going with ya'll story, and Tim wants me to send them when I'm done."

"So you're gonna be my writer then huh?" I asked.

"I guess so, because he's really interested in hearing about male strippers and how you decided ta jump in this line of business," she replied.

"Cool, when's a good time for us to meet up?" I asked.

"How bout Monday? I'm free and I've already finished up my last column to free me up to get you guy's story." "That'll be fine. I've got a few more things I'd like to run by you if you don't mind. See you Monday," I said, and hung up.

I was happy that shit was taking off fast and I wasn't planning on fucking my way to success, but they say sometimes you gotta make sacrifices. But I knew I had to be careful too because I was playing a dangerous game.

I texted Red to see if he still wanted to invest and he shot back *Yeah*, so I told him I'd get at him when I was gonna send some guys on a road trip.

After that I went and delivered the news to Sunni. Babygirl is propped up beside her and the movie was just now going off.

"Damn! I missed it!" I said, tryna sound disappointed.

"You didn't wanna watch it," Sunni said with a smirk. I just laughed.

"Babygirl, go get ready for bed." It was about 9 PM and I had to be up early, and we had dinner at Mama G's too.

After Babygirl headed to her room to shower and get ready for bed, I gave Sunni the news and she jumped in my arms and wrapped her legs around my waist and kissed me deeply.

I sat her back on her feet and let her know we'd have to take a rain check on the love making. She pouted and headed toward the room. I went to the kitchen to get me something to drink before following her to the bedroom.

Sunni was reading a book. "Whatcha reading bae?" I asked.

"About a dude named Shawn from Lil Rock who grew up poor and got rich outta nowhere," she replied, not taking her eyes off her book.

"That's gonna be me real soon," I tell her, climbing in the bed and plugging my phone up on the nightstand.

She dogeared the corner page and put it down before hitting the light and cuddling up to me. Instantly we dozed off because I been running the streets all day.

8

I WOKE UP EARLY SUNDAY morning and thought, *Damn I gotta lotta shit to do today.*

I rolled over, pulling myself free of Sunni and looked at the clock. It was 7:17 AM and I had to get a move on. I jumped up and got me a quick shower, shave, and hit my grill. After stepping out the bathroom, Sunni was still deep in her sleep.

"Time to rise and shine bae," I said, slapping her on the ass.

"Mmmm...you already owe me!" she said, moaning from the love tap I gave her.

"I got you bae, promise," I told her. "And besides, I've got sum to show ya'll so get up bae. We'll get breakfast on the way out," I told her, leaving out the room to go wake Babygirl.

I got to her door and looked in at her sleeping. She looked just like her momma Myka and I can't front, I missed her a lot, but we gotta move on.

I went in and shook Babygirl awake.

"Rise n' shine princess. Get you a shower and dress comfortable because it's supposed to be hot today," I told her, kissing her forehead and walking out. I grabbed my phone and went to the living room to watch TV, waiting on the women to get ready.

It was gonna be hot, so I donned some Levi shorts, huaraches, and a white Nike v-neck t-shirt. After about 30 minutes they both came out with they long hair in a ponytail, shorts, and Polo shirts. Babygirl had on flip flops and Sunni had on a pair of retro Jordan's. The only difference between their outfits was their shirts; Babygirl had on a striped white and pink Polo and Sunni had on a red Polo.

"Ya'll ready?" I asked.

"Yeah, what's for breakfast?" Babygirl asked.

"We gonna stop and get something to eat on our way out," I told her and ushered them to the door.

"Where we going E?" Sunni asked.

"You'll see, just be patient," I told her. Grabbing my keys, we headed out and I locked up behind us. It was only 8 AM and the heat was already suffocating. I hit the alarm, unlocking the car, and hurried and jumped in to start the A/C.

"Dang! It's hot as hell out here!" Sunni said. I rolled down the windows and let the sunroof back in the BMW. The car reeked of weed and black magic air freshener. Sunni leaned over in my ear.

"You been smoking E?"

"A lil bit, but I promise to stop before the baby's born," I whispered back. She just put her hand up in my face like, "Miss me with that shit." I didn't say nothing. I just turned on Power 92 and pulled out the driveway.

After picking up some breakfast sandwiches at Micky D's, we pulled up at this big ass house in M—off a street called High Timber Drive. "Who lives here daddy?" Babygirl asked, finishing up her breakfast.

"Yeah, who's house is this, Evan?" Sunni said, still ticked off.

"Hopefully ours one day," I replied, unbuckling my seatbelt

and stepping out. Babygirl ran to the house and went in.

"E, have you lost your mind? We don't have the money for a big ass house like this. Are you crazy!?" Sunni fumed.

"Calm the fuck down, I said 'one day,' you act like a nigga gonna buy it now and if I did what you mad for? It's more room for us!" I replied, getting heated. I walked off to go find my daughter.

It was an open house, so when I stepped in the air was flowing and the foyer was big. I walked to the back patio where I heard Babygirl still admiring the house.

I heard the front door close as I stepped out the back. The house was huge and cost a lot, but after the money I made and the little investments I'ma put up, we'd be straight.

"Daddy! Look at this pool!" Babygirl said excitedly.

"Yeah it's real nice," I replied, hugging her to my side and looking around the big backyard that was gated in.

"Damn, this is very nice," Sunni said, admiring the house too.

"Told ya," I said, giving her a devilish smirk. "Let's go because we got a lot to do today," I said, heading for the front.

We got back in the car, I had left it running to keep the leather cool in the hundred degree weather. We looked at a few more houses before leaving, just driving by before heading out. My phone vibrated and the screen read "Ms. D."

I answered, "What's good ma?"

"Just moving around. When you coming through?" she asked.

"We on our way now," I replied.

"Who's we!?" she yelled into the phone.

"Man, I got Sunni and my daughter with me. I'll be pulling up in a few," I told her and hung up.

"Where we going now Daddy?" Babygirl asked.

"Gotta handle something, so sit back and ride. Ya'll with

Daddy today," I told her, and crunk the music up hitting I-40 headed to North Little Rock.

Ms. D

This nigga really had me fucked up! He still owes me some dick, and on top of that he bringing this bitch and daughter to my house.

Well, I'ma show her why that was a big mistake. I'ma make sure this nigga leaves with me on his mind with a hard dick. He just betta remember what bitch helped him get this shit off the ground. But I got em tho.

I had seen Lil Jon earlier and we were on the same page. It didn't matter that he was put away right now, his mind was still on business, and that's why I'd come to work for him. All I had to do was make sure we had Big E under control.

I looked at the time, it was after 9 AM and from the sound of it, he wasn't too far away. But I had a trick for this nigga for real. I jumped in the shower and put my thoughts on something else.

Big E

Pulling up at Ms. D's spot, her Lexus and Kim's Jeep was in the drive. I told Babygirl and Sunni they didn't have to wait in the car, so they got out and followed me to the front door. I pulled my key out and Sunni leaned and whispered in my ear, "You got keys to this bitch's house now!?"

I just shook my head; Sunni was really starting to piss me off today. We stepped out the heat into the air conditioned house. Tana looked up as we came into the living room.

"Wassup E? Didn't know you were stopping by," she said, with a questioning look.

"Yeah, gotta look at some shit D wants me to check out," I replied.

"Aww, who's this princess you got with you?" Tana asked, smiling at Babygirl.

"Oh this is my daughter, Babygirl, and my Mrs. Barrow. Her name's Sunni," I said, introducing her to my daughter and girl.

"Aww. She's so beautiful. Do you like playing Candy Crush?" Tana asked Babygirl.

"Yeah, but I play Angry Birds a lot," she replied.

"You can go play with her while I talk to Sunni real quick and handle some business," I told Babygirl, and directed Sunni toward the kitchen.

In the kitchen, she said, "E, whatchu got –"

"Aye, check this out. Dis is where I started my business, and this is also where my little brotha laid his head before he got locked up. So don't come questioning me how I conduct my business," I said, cutting her off.

Sunni was quiet for a moment. "I'm sorry bae, I didn't mean it like that. Being pregnant has me moody. I'm sorry daddy," she said, hugging and kissing me.

I returned both and we headed back to the living room where Tana and Babygirl sat glued to Tana's iPad.

"I'll be right back. You ladies play nicely," I said, heading toward the back room.

I stepped in the guest room where Kim and Ms. D was at. D's hair was up in a bun, she had on these tight ass shorts and some yellow and black Pumas with a matching top. That ass look like it grew overnight. She look like she was fresh from a shower. Kim was in her usual, she was rocking a Nike fit with some Guess jeans. She looked damn good too.

"Hey E! I didn't hear you come in," Kim said, turning around and hanging up the phone.

"I just made it, but what's good?" I asked her and D as she turned around from the computer.

"I'll let D explain everything," Kim said.

"Yeah, can you give us a minute to talk anyway?" Ms. D asked and Kim got the hint, grabbed her phone, and headed out the room.

Ms. D followed her to the door and locked it tryna be slick. When she turned around she had an evil smirk on her face.

"Wassup ma?" I asked, leaning on the desk.

"Nigga you know what it is!" she shot back, and before I knew it she was across the room and in my arms with our lips locked and our tongues tied.

"Ma, you trippin! My girl in the living room."

"So? The door locked!" she shot back.

I palmed that ass and pushed her back.

"Nigga, and besides, you owe me anyways!" and with that she dropped to her knees and began unbuckling my pants.

I tried to fight her off, she knew I wanted it just as bad as she did. She pulled my semi erect dick out and began to stroke me to life. She swallowed my whole length and after about ten minutes, I came long and hard and she milked me to the last drop.

I was damn near about to buckle at the knees, so I hurried up and tucked my soft dick back in my pants.

She got herself together before unlocking the door and telling Kim to come back in the room. If Kim was outside the door that means she knew what was up, and she gave me a look when she came back in like they had one up on me. I liked Ms. D, but I didn't like the feeling that I was being played, and I was starting to wonder why Ms. D was so interested in me when she clearly had other niggas around.

"But like I said E, I called your guy Red in Chicago and he agreed to come down here instead," Ms. D said, like we were talking business while Kim was out the room.

"Aight, and my homeboy Rudy supposed to be getting at you too bout a job. The guys I'm waiting on supposed to get at me when they step out the pen," I told her.

"Alright. I'll be waiting on him and anyways, let's go meet your girl and daughter."

So me, Ms. D and Kim all step into the living room, and Babygirl, Tana and Sunni were all tuned into Tana's I-Pad. Babygirl was in the middle holding it.

"You ladies getting along here?" I asked, making all three of them jump.

"Hey babe! Your daughter's really smart, E. You need to sit down and watch her on my i-Pad at home," Sunni said, and I leaned over to see what they were doing. Babygirl was designing a photo of her, Sunni and Tana.

"That looks interesting, but bae this is Deedra, but we call her Ms. D, and that's Kim," I said, introducing them.

"Bae Tana explained to me in so many words about the club and stuff and I think I want to contribute too," Sunni said.

"Aight bae, we'll see," I told her. "Let me call Kay. I need her over here."

After getting off the phone with Kay, I told Tana and Kim to set Babygirl up in Tana's room with a movie and some snacks. Babygirl agreed and followed them happily to the kitchen. I looked at Sunni.

"Now how you gonna work for the club, pregnant, and watch Babygirl?" I asked. Ms. D's face went pale when I said pregnant.

"E, my sister lives nearby and got two lil girls too," she replied.

"Aw okay if that's what you wanna do. We'll find a place to put you bae. Just be patient," I told her, and D's phone began to ring.

"E, Red's on the phone," Ms. D said. I grabbed the phone.

"What's good bro? I've been waiting on your call," I said to Red, stepping outside and leaving Ms. D and Sunni in the living room talking. It was hella hot, so I just stood under the porch shade.

"Yeah I got your message and I'd be down with coming down there too, just send a nigga the address and I'll be on the first thang smoking to the A, but when I'm done you know you gotta come up here and show these ladies some love too," he replied.

"Oh that's no doubt! We can set that up when you get here. I'll text you the info you need and I'll see ya next week."

"Aight, bet that. Just remember, the windy city got a lotta love to show you and ya guys," he said.

"Red, I gotchu." And we disconnected the call. I was already anxious to see what my nigga Red had in store for me up there. I hurried out the heat and Tana passed me on her way out.

In the living room Sunni and Ms. D were looking at something on the iPad. I leaned in and see they just browsing through photos and comments on Facebook and Instagram.

"Bae, did you see the show you guys put on Friday night?" Sunni asked.

"Nah, that must've been some side shit?" I replied.

"Yeah it was, but that was some I sent Raheem and Sam on. Some of my homegirls in Conway were freaky and looking for a show, but don't worry, we split the profits. It was more than just dancing involved. I bet them niggas came back with almost 2k!" Ms. D said excitedly.

She handed me a wad of hunnid dollar bills. "Here's $500 to go in the pile."

"Cool, preciate that ma." On perfect timing Tana came back in with mail and Kay was right behind her.

"Wassup bro!" Kay said, giving me a hug, then greeting the rest of the women in the room. Tana handed me a letter and it was from my nigga JD.

"Not shit, tryna get everything in line," I told her, reading JD's letter. He informed me he'd be home next week and that was good because I'd have some shit set up by then.

"But aye, check this out. When we start going from state to state, Kay, you and Sunni will be in charge of making sure the guys get to and from the airport. Sunni, when the club opens, you'll be working in there. Ms. D, you're a business partner, so just keep me informed

on what you, Tana and Kim got for us. The next step ladies is LA!" I said and they all nodded in unison.

"Sunni and anotha thing, call Gee and let him know where him and BG need to be. I'll be around too, so let's get dis money ladies!" I sang out, and they all laughed. I asked Sunni if she wanted to go with me and she said she was gonna stay with Kay, and she'd bring her home.

"Well I'ma go by the house and handle some shit real quick," I told her, and headed for the door. I called Gee before getting in the car.

"Wassup E?" he answered.

"Not shit. Have you talked to that nigga Black?" I asked.

"Yeah, earlier, why wassup?"

"Nothing, he got a new number. Get at him and tell him to get at me real quick." I told him.

"Bet" he said and hung up. I jumped in my BMW and thought it was time for an upgrade, but I'd worry bout that later. I pulled out and headed for the highway home thinking bout the long road to success.

Raheem

I pulled up at PJ's to see what was jumpin. I left Keisha's ass home because she was trippin and I didn't feel like dealing with her right now.

I had that "Handsome and Wealthy" by Migos bumping on my new Panasonic flip screen in dash. I'd just washed my Chevy, got a fresh tapper, and jumped down fresh. When I was working at the prison, I had stacked my bread and put everything back just in case really.

I donned a pair of pressed True Religion jeans, blue and white Airmax 90s, and a white Polo shirt. It was cool outside, the sun had went down, but it was still humid. It was still early a lil after 7 and it was a lil packed.

I shook some hands and gave some females a nod. I went to the bar and ordered me a vodka and OJ. Something light and cheap because I had a lot of moves to make later on.

There was a few females here and there dancing, all in nigga's faces seeking attention, but I'd dismiss a thirsty ass female quick and I'm really on the verge of dismissing Keisha soon, because I got my eye on that bigger picture and fuckin with her wasn't going to cut it.

"Get down Heem!" somebody yelled, drawing me outta my thoughts. Turning around, my niggas Sam and Stephon were at a table talking to some females. I made my way over to the table to chill for a minute.

"What's up wit ya'll?" I asked, taking a seat beside this thick red bone who looked like she could be Keisha Cole's twin, some gap and everything.

"Man, taking a break before we head to this address E's homegirl sent," Sam said.

"Aww cool. So what ya'll do at PJ's?" I asked.

"Getting us a quick drank and talking bout the lil money

we been making here and there," Stephon said.

"Cool, cool. I really just swung by to see what was jumpin. But ya'll niggas take it easy, if ya'll need an extra hand get at me," I said, downing my drink and rising to leave.

"Man, hol' up. Check this out. When you think this shit gonna jump off? We been working for E for a lil second and the money we making going straight to him opening a club," Steph said.

"Man, I don't know but we gonna be straight. I got faith in his moves. He seems like a real man of business," I replied.

"Alright, we'll ride with you for now, and see what it looks like later on," Steph said. I nodded and rose to leave, shaking my nigga's hands and making my way to my ride.

"Umm..excuse me?" I heard a high pitched voice behind me call. I turned to see the red bone with red hair. She rocked some tight ass blue jean shorts that was tight round the thighs, this diamond collar shirt, yellow and white and some yellow and white spartan sandals that went up her tatted calves.

"Yeah wassup ma?" I asked, turning round.

Standing up she was about 5'5" and thicker than I thought and bow legged.

"Umm...my name is Sasha, but my homegirls call me Red. I'm tryna see if you do the same thing yo friends do?" she asked.

Now, this is what you would call a bad bitch.

"Yeah, why, wassup?" I asked in return.

"Shit, I want you to do a show for me my nigga, is that gonna be a problem?" she asked with a lil cockiness.

"Nah, why don't you take down my numba and we can set some up."

"Aight, that's cool, but I want some of yo time tonight," she said.

"I can do that, but my time cost too," I told her.

"That won't be a problem," she replied, reaching in her back pocket coming out with a folded wad of bills.

I counted out $500 in fresh hunnid dolla bills, my eyes got big.

"Yeah, a bitch papered up, and that's for your time. Now for my show. I get you if my show is good?" she said with a questioning look.

"Yeah...yeah, I got you," I said. "Is it gonna be jus you?" I asked.

"Yeah, so come prepared," she said, and gave me her number and walked back to the club, throwing that ass extra hard before disappearing inside. I walked to my Chevy. This female had a nigga hard already. I texted her and let her know it was me and I'd see her around 11:30 tonight.

She replied, *Bet, I'll be waiting, so bring ya A-game. And everyone calls me Diamond.* I keyed her in and jumped in my ride to handle some B.I. before my lil meeting with Diamond lata ta'night. I pulled off smiling.

Big E

It was a little after 8:45 when Babygirl and Sunni walked in the house followed by Kay. I'd just got done putting a meal together for them. I gave the guys a call before they walked in and was just now getting off my phone.

They'd already been to the gym and was heading to a show now.

"Damn bae! Sum' smells good," Sunni said.

"Yeah I'm putting together a tater tot casserole with extra cheese," I said.

"Well I'm sho hungry," Kay said.

"You're welcome to stay," I told Kay.

"Nah, I got some shit to handle. I just wanted ta make sure

ya ladies got home safe," Kay told me.

"Alright, bet. Call me if you need something sis," I told Kay. I gave my sister a hug and let her out. On my way to the kitchen my phone vibrated. It was a number I didn't know.

"Yeah?" I answered.

"Wassup E. This Black, Gee told me to call you," Black said.

"Yeah, I need another like the otha," I told him.

"I gotchu shit, where you at now?" Black asked.

"I'm at the house now. I see you gotta new numba. I'ma key you in and text you the address."

"Cool, I'll drop that off. I'm heading to a freak Nick in Georgia, so I'll be through in a few," Black said, and we hung up.

I went back to the kitchen to fix plates. Babygirl was in the living room on her phone and Sunni was sitting at the table on her I-Pad.

"Bae ya'll got a lotta followers now, and majority of them are outta state," Sunni said as I began making plates. After bout 15 minutes I called Babygirl to come eat right as I heard a knock at the door. I set the plates down and went to answer the door.

The nigga Black was indeed black as hell, so I see why they call him that.

"Wassup my dude?" I asked, shaking his hand.

"Not shit bruh, just came to drop this off before heading out."

"A'righty, take it easy and be careful on the highway," I told him, and walked back in out of the Sunday night heat. I pocket the weed to be sure Sunni or Babygirl didn't see it. Back in the kitchen, the girls were having a good laugh.

"And what's so funny?" I asked.

They stayed on their phones or tablets doing something

or watching something. I left them alone and ate my food thinking bout everything I had left to do. I still had to find me a building and get things together for this magazine interview.

I finished my food as the girls made their way to their rooms, then cleaned up the kitchen and retreated to our bedroom. I looked in on Babygirl and made sure she plugged her phone up and went to bed before 10 PM, and closed her door.

In our bedroom Sunni was laying down looking like she was fresh out of the shower. I climbed in bed and laid next to her as she turned off the TV and light and we laid there talking before we finally dozed off.

Raheem

It was nearing 11 PM when my phone vibrated. It was a text from Diamond: *You didn't change ya mind did ya?*

Nah, I'ma swang by the crib and freshen up then I'ma be on my way, I replied.

A minute later, *Okay*, was her only reply.

I had bent a few corners and chilled at the Lake Saracen for a minute and ended up staying there throughout the day. Thought about going to the port but said fuck it. Keisha had been blowing my shit up all day, but I was ignoring her because I was ready to let this bitch out. When I pulled up, I didn't see her Maxima out front, so that was a relief.

I parked and dashed up to my condo real quick to get me a quick shower and overnight bag just in case. After my shower, I heard my phone vibratin' hard against the counter. It was another text from Diamond: *You sure you still coming?*

Yeah, I'm getting dressed now, text me the addy and I'll be there, I replied. She texted me the info and I noticed that she lived by the Lake, so she had to have a lil bread living in this part of town.

I dressed down in a pair of Jordan shorts, a black Jordan shirt with the blue jump man, and some blue, black, and white retros. I sprayed on some of that Creed, gave myself a once over, grabbed my bag, and headed out. On my way out the building Keisha was pulling up.

"Where da fuck you going hmm?" she said, angry and looking like she was bout to bust a blood vessel.

"Heading outta town with the fellas, so I need my spot empty till I come back, and when I come back," I replied. She knew I didn't raise my voice, but I didn't like being followed or watched.

"Raheem whatchu saying!?" she cried out.

"Don't be here when I get back." And with that I climbed in my Chevy and pulled out.

I texted Diamond and told her I was on the way and asked did I need to bring anything. She replied, saying, *Energy and an appetite*. I smiled big because it's been a while since I had a woman seeking my attention.

I was only 26 and was doing good for myself. I bumped that "Kickin Shit" by Quando Rondo on my way to Diamond's crib. It was only a 15 minute drive and when I pulled up the neighborhood was quiet and her house was right on the lake. I left my bag in the car, because I didn't wanna be the one to make the first move.

I made it to the wooden door and knocked a couple times before it popped open. Diamond looked hella sexy tonight. She donned a white bottom lingerie, a white tank top that was damn near see through, with her nipples erect as the night breeze hit her.

"Damn! You lookin hella beautiful, ma," I told her, complimenting her womanly figure.

"And you smell hella good and look good too," she replied. I just nodded and she stepped back and invited me into the house.

Her lake house was real nice, she had a suede all white furniture set, the big couch was a wrap around and a small loveseat. It was a staircase off the living room in the hallway. She had a wooden coffee table that had a maroon-ish red tint, and her 60 inch LG flatscreen and entertainment center was hittin' too.

"Damn ma, you got a nice home," I told her.

"Thank you, you can kick back and get comfy. I don't bite," she replied, walking outta the room an disappearing up the hall.

I walked around the room one time and ducked my head into a closed over door. On the other side was a huge office with floor to ceiling lights and the newest computer setup. The computer chair and a large L-shaped sofa were black leather. Ma wasn't kidding when it came to business I could tell; she was professional as hell.

I walked back into the living room and grabbed the remote off the table and began channel surfing, and a few minutes later Diamond popped back up.

"Do you like pasta and garlic bread?" she asked, holdin a hot spoon with a towel under it.

"Yeah! It smells hella good," I replied.

"Taste this good," she said, leaning over and exposing the top of her breasts to me. I blew on the red sauce before tasting it. Still hot, but damn good.

"Mmmm…That's good! What is it?" I asked, standing up.

"Family recipe. Why don't you come in here and join me at the bar?" she said and turned around. I admired her curves as she walked off and finally noticed the vine of tiger lilies tatted up both thighs. The woman had an ass like a horse, and threw it side to side like she knew a nigga scopin her out.

I followed her to the kitchen and when I stepped in, I was in awe of the shit I seen. Everything was top notch.

"Damn! Now this kitchen is nice as hell too!" I told her. She just giggled.

"Would you like sum to drink?" she asked.

"Shit, whatever you hav'n I'm hav'n," I told her, and she smiled at me, turned, and pulled down two wine glasses. My eyes never left her ass.

Outside of the daisy dukes you can see her real curves, and she was very curvaceous, but it was something bout her that set a nigga on edge. So I kept my guard up because a woman this damn fine — it was trouble prone to follow. I watched as she poured our glasses. She picked up her glass and gave a quick sniff before raising her glass for a toast.

"To a wonderful night," she said, as I gave her glass a small clink and took a sip.

A nigga didn't drink wine, let alone outta wine glasses. So a nigga really felt on top right now.

"Ma, I got a question. Outta all the ballas in the club, you set ya eyes on me. Why?" I asked.

She set her glass down, turned the stove down, and came around the bar to me. "For one, ya friends was talking bout you before you came in, and when you came in, I knew I wanted a dance from you. And besides, a bitch single and ready to mingle. The way you moved is what attracted me to you. So does that answer ya question?" she shot back.

I turned to face her and she stepped between my legs.

"Yeah, I guess," I said with a light chuckle. She wrapped my hands around her waist and I inhaled her sweet Paris Hilton perfume. Her hazel eyes were beautiful and everything about this woman screamed Boss Bitch. I liked that.

"Well dinner's ready and I figured we could take our meals

on the back patio to look at the lake. And don't worry, a bitch gotsa mosquito net up," she said as she began making plates. We took our glasses of wine and pasta to the back patio, where it was cool.

She had small candles lit, and this futon out back that we relaxed and ate on. We exchanged convo between eating, and that's how I found out she was an only child and worked in real estate. So that explained the house and the Mercedes out front.

"So you're in this stripping game now?" she asked, turning toward me after she put her plate down.

"Yeah, I am. I got brought into it by a friend. My man Big E just started it up after getting out the pen."

Diamond eyed me up and down. "Well you certainly have the build for the job. But let me ask you this — what makes you think this business is gonna succeed? Especially when the man running things has been locked up."

I shook my head. "You don't know E," I told her. "Trust me, he's a leader. Whatever he sets his mind to, I'm sure he's gonna succeed. You should see the cash we already got after just a few weeks of working. And we ain't even set up for the real business yet — we're just trying to make enough to get this thing off the ground."

Diamond was eyeing me in a way that made me wish I had talked less about E and his plans. But she looked down and ran her hand along my thigh, and I forgot all about those worries.

After our meal we reclined on the futon and talked. She cuddled up to me and I wrapped her up.

"So how old are you, if you don't mind me asking?" I asked.

"I'm 36, and no I don't mind. How bout yourself?" she asked in return.

"You got me by 10, ma," I replied.

"Damn! I got me a baby!" she said and we busted out laughing.

"So you in your own business?" I asked her, trying to be polite — after all, she was paying me a good amount of money. It was about the company and conversation as well.

"Mmm," Diamond murmured against my mouth, pulling back from a kiss. "Yeah. I been at it since I was younger than you. Worked for other people first, and then started up on my own as soon as I could. I do pretty well for myself as an agent, I know talent when I see it."

She ran a finger down my chest teasingly.

After we calmed down I tilted her chin up and gave those juicy lips a small peck before she rolled on top and kissed me deep.

She pushed past my lips with her tongue and our tongues made connection. Her mouth tasted sweet from the wine and her lips were as soft as I had imagined.

She broke the kiss, leaned up, and took off her muscle shirt. Her titties were perfect. They were at least Ds, her nipples were erect from the cool air, and her areolas were caramel brown.

"Damn, you sexy as hell," I told her. I leaned up and locked lips with the left nipple and stroked the right one.

"Mmmm…Papi, just like that!" she purred, and that's when I noticed she had a slight accent. I kicked my J's off and continued to kiss and suck on her luscious breasts. We got up to stretch the futon out and I laid down on top of her but she stopped me.

"You gotta strip for me papi," she said, that sexy Spanish accent coming out more. She grabbed a remote and pressed a button and soft music began to play. I stripped for her until I got to my boxers.

She seen my semi hardness and her eyes got big. She licked her lips as I stood in front of her. She leaned up and pulled my boxers down to release my dick.

"Damn Papi, you part horse or something!?" she asked, stroking me slowly, then wrapping her thick lips around the head, drawing a growl from me. She began to deep throat me for a minute and she had a no gag reflex. I felt my nuts get tight and I guess she did too, because she released me, leaned back, and pulled her panties off.

Everything about this woman was beautiful, even that pussy. She had a gold ring in her clit hood and her clit stuck out a little, letting me know she was ready for me. I kicked off my boxers and climbed between her open legs and she grabbed ahold of my erection and rubbed me up and down her clit.

"Damn papi, you so big, so be gentle with me because I'm very valuable," she said.

"I got you ma," I replied, and pushed forward as she guided me toward her juicy wetness. She was hella tight and by the time I fought my way in I was ready to cum. I knew I had to hit this again but for now, I'ma enjoy this shit!

9

Big E

IT WAS 10:47 ON MONDAY morning when I got up and the house was still quiet. Sunni was still passed out next to me and I was guessing Babygirl was still asleep too. I had to hit the fellas up and see what they made over the weekend.

I rolled out the bed, grabbed me a quick shower, brushed my teeth, and got dressed. Sunni's phone went off on the nightstand and I glanced over to see a number I didn't recognize and the message *Are you sure?*

That was suspicious as hell, but when I looked at her all tucked up in our bed with her hand curled over her stomach protectively, the frown melted off my face. Sunni had been by my side even when I was locked up and I was sure she was loyal to me.

It was supposed to rain today, so I just threw on some jeans, a pair of Nike boots, and a black pull over. I grabbed my phone, kissed Sunni, and stepped out the room.

I peeked in on Babygirl before going to the living room. I

called my guy Gee first. He answered on the 2nd ring.

"Was good E?" he asked.

"Man, not too much of shit. Jus' getting outta bed and was about to try to see what the weekend brought in," I told him.

"Shit, already collected. We made over 2K this week. I'm on my way to ya spot now."

"Aight cool. I'ma be waiting on you," I told him and hung up. I cut the TV on and surfed through channels. I heard a car pull up about 20 minutes later, than a knock at the door.

I answered the door and stepped out on the porch with Gee.

"Bruh, let's take a ride," I told him, and we hopped in his truck. I pulled up in the passenger seat and fired up.

"So how'd the ladies take to BG?" I asked, talking a hit of the blunt and holding it in.

"Awww shit, bruh was shy at first, but he broke loose after a few drunks and some weed."

"That's wassup, but it's time to up the stakes bro. I don't wanna rush the shit, but we gotta get us a building and get this shit jumpin," I told him, passing him the blunt.

"Yeah, it's bout that time," he replied, inhaling the smoke.

"I gotta get the storyline together for the magazine shoot. We already got some pictures for it, just need my opening now."

"Well let's stop bullshittin and half steppin and get on it," he replied, passing the end of the joint.

"Bet," was all I said.

We pulled back up to my spot, from turning corners and smoking this pressure Black brought through, he handed me the roll of money. I gave my guy some dap and stepped out and ran to the front door in the rain. Walking in the house, I heard movement in the kitchen. I walked in and Sunni was preparing to cook something.

"Wassup bae, whatchu making?" I asked, walking up behind her and kissing her cheek. She pulled away from me.

"You been smokin?' she asked with a mug on her face.

"Yeah, a lil bit."

"Well don't come by me smelling like that bullshit E!"

"Aight I gotchu but put that up and go get dressed. It's Monday morning. I'm taking ya'll out to eat," I told her. She started putting everything up and I went to spray on some cologne. I woke Babygirl on my way to the room and told her to get up and get herself together.

After everyone was up and dressed I unlocked the car from the house and started it. They ran to the car while I locked up the house. In the car, Sunni was playing with the radio and Babygirl was looking out the window.

"Where you wanna eat breakfast, Babygirl?" I asked.

"Ummm...I never ate at I-Hop. Can we go there?" she asked.

"Yeah, that's perfect. They got some chocolate chip pancakes I wanna try," I told her with a smile. "Be right back," I said, taking my key to get back in the house. I'd forgot to grab some money out the safe. I was in and out in a few minutes and we were off.

I grabbed 5K from the safe just in case and now we were headed to breakfast and hopefully by the time we got to I-Hop, Sunni would have a change of attitude.

Raheem

I felt something on my dick that brought me outta a good sleep. I looked down to see Diamond giving me a good wake up call.

"Damn ma! Now that's whatchu call an alarm clock," I said with a deep groan and fell back on these fluffy ass pillows.

We fucked all over the house last night and finally made it to the bedroom upstairs. I was enjoying the head, and came long and hard. She cleaned me up and gave my dick one last long hard suck before swallowing all my cum and jumping out the bed, heading toward the shower.

"Time ta get up Papi!" she sang out behind the bathroom door.

I laid back for a minute, then jumped up, put my shorts on, grabbed my keys and headed to my car to get my overnight bag. It was raining, so I dashed out and in the house. When I made it back upstairs she was still in the shower. I looked at the clock on the nightstand and it read 11 AM.

Me and Diamond didn't pass out until about 2 AM the night before. I dropped my shorts and bag and headed to the bathroom. In the glass case walk-in shower Diamond looked so damn sexy.

"You came to join me finally?" she asked with a smirk. She had her head back, water running down them big ass titties, and in the light her pussy looked more beautiful than my first glance at it. My dick instantly rose to attention.

"Woah Papi! Stand down!" she said, smiling real big.

"I guess I can spare you right now," I told her, smiling back. I stepped in the hot shower with her and began to soap up as she rinsed off, gave my dick a light tug and stroke, and stepped out. I switched on the cold shower and cooled myself down, but it was still something bout Diamond that set me on edge.

I rinsed off and cut the shower and stepped out. When I towel dried and came out the bathroom she was hanging up her phone.

"You good Papi?" she asked, still naked.

"Nah, you need to get some clothes on or we gonna need another shower," I told her and we busted out laughing.

"And you too! But I got something for you and since ya car blocking me in we can take yo ride to handle my business, and have hands too?" she asked.

"Cool," I replied. We finished getting ready.

Since it was raining outside she put on a pair of tight fitted jeans, some Timberland boots, a long sleeve Nike shirt with a hoodie. I'm glad I brought a pair of jeans with me. Didn't have shit else to do today. So I didn't bring nun to dress down in, but a t-shirt, jeans, and Jordan's. I kept my jacket in the car.

"You ready ma?" I asked, coming back into the room.

"Yep. Let me grab some shit and I'll meet you at the car," she said.

"Bet," I told her. I grabbed my keys and phone and headed to the car. I checked my phone and had a few texts and calls from Keisha and a call from Big E.

I re-dialed Big E.

"Wassup witcha Yougnsta,?" E answered.

"Not shit, just pulled an all nigtha with an older chick and she bad too, E," I replied.

"Awrighty. You ain't do no shows this weekend?"

"Nah, Steph an the guys told me they got everything handled. But the female I stayed with last night wanted a private dance and paid me in advance."

"Aww shit you straight. Ya might need to hang on to that chick them," E said.

"Yeah, you know I am, but I'ma pull up on you lata with some bread when I get done taking her around," I told E.

"Aight, just get at me later."

"Aye. Here she comes, I'ma hitcha back lata," I said, cutting E off.

"Aight," and we disconnected the call. She got in the car and that Paris Hilton hit me in the nose.

"You already to go, ma?" I asked when she settled in with her Chanel clutch.

"Yup, and you keep your car clean for it to be a classic," she replied. I was kinda shocked that she even knew my Caprice was a classic.

"Yeah, my father was a mechanic, so I grew up learning bout cars," she added.

"Tha's wassup. So where we headed to?" I asked.

"First let's go eat because a bitch hungry afta last night. I can eat a full course meal by myself," she said, and I laughed. I crunk up that "No Days Off" by Fetty Wap and she smiled and leaned back as I turned up the music and let my 12s beat against the seat. We headed for lunch and to run around.

Big E

We finished eating and sat in I-Hop talking about my plans going to LA for the magazine shoot, everything. Sunday we had to go to Sunni's parents for dinner and after that I had to go see Lil Jon.

"I'ma put Red up at Lil Jon's other house and put it in my name as well," I told Sunni. Babygirl was busy on her phone like all kids her age now.

"That's straight too bae," Sunni replied.

"Let's get outta here," I said. I dropped a fifty on my ticket on the table and we headed out the door. It had stopped raining and the sun came out and it was already heating up outside. Then it hit me that I was 'pose to meet the guys at the gym Sunday.

Right as I pulled my phone out to call Gee, it vibrated in my hand and his name popped up on the screen.

"Damn bruh, I forgot to meet ya'll at the gym last night. My bad," I said, answering the phone.

"E, you got a lot to do. Don't stress it fam. I got these niggas, you jus handle yo end and get this shit jumpin," Gee said.

"Aight bro, I preciate it. I'ma keep in touch. Ya'll just make sho ya'll stay in touch with D and the girls."

"I gotchu E, but I got some shit jumpin right now. I'ma hit you back later this week," Gee said.

"Aight bruh, stay up," and we hung up the phone. We climbed in the car and headed for Kay's house for a lil bit.

Raheem

It was a lil afta 2 PM and it was heating up afta it stopped raining. I was enjoying the day wit Diamond. She was a cool ass female, to be 10 years older than me. We stopped at a few places and she holla'd at a few females and came back to the car.

"Where to now ma?" I asked when she got back in the car.

"Back to the house for a minute. Let's get out this humid ass heat," she replied.

"Aight," I said, heading back to Lake Saracen.

We made it back to her spot and it was bout 2:37 PM and it seemed to have gotten even hotta outside. She darted through the front door, threw her keys, clutch, and phone on her couch, and jetted upstairs.

"Taking a shower Papi, you care to join me?" she asked.

"Yeah, then a nigga got some B.I. ta handle," I told her, getting naked on my way to the shower.

By the time we made it upstairs to her room, she was already naked and in the bathroom. I dicked her down in the shower for about an hour and a half. We dried off, put on some clean cool clothes, and I packed my bag.

She handed me a small white envelope and told me to call her when I made it home. I agreed, she walked me to the front door.

Before I walked out I promised her I'd hit her up later

when I got home. I checked my phone when I got in the car. I had a lot of missed calls from Keisha, and some of my niggas. I'd hit them up later when I got home and chilled for a minute.

I opened the envelope she gave me and inside was straight hunnid dolla bills with a little note that read: *Heem, I enjoyed your company and wish to see more of you. Enjoy this, and if we connect how I'd like, there's more where that came from.*

She had signed it Diamond. I counted out 15 hunnid dollars. I don't know if lil mama was crazy or what, but I was sure to find out.

I fired up the Chevy and backed out, heading cross town in the afternoon heat and traffic.

Big E

We pulled up at Kay's and the neighborhood was quiet. Hell that's a first in John Barrow. It's normally something going on out here, but I wasn't gonna let that stop me from getting on my grind. Kay had a few cars in the driveway so I parked on the street.

It was still humid outside since it had rained earlier in the day. We got out and headed to the house with Babygirl and Sunni on my heels. She was starting to get in her feelings, and becoming real moody lately, and that shit was driving me. I knocked once and walked in.

You could hear talking in the living room and we headed in that direction. Kay was staring at a laptop on her coffee table with her friends sitting beside her.

"Oh hey brotha! I was just showing the ladies some of ya latest work," Kay said.

"That's wassup, and I also need you to do a lil recruitment for me while you on there too. I'm having an audition on June 1st and you ladies will be the judges," I replied.

"Ohhhh shit! This is gonna be fun!" Kay said.

"Yeah, but that's all I need for now — and to stop and check on you. But we been out all morning, I'm a get up with you lata, Kay," I told her before heading to the door.

In the car I checked my phone and had a message from Raheem and Shonequa. I disregarded them until I got home. A nigga had to admit, tryna run a business was harder than I thought. We jumped in the car and headed back to Sunni's house in Dumas.

My phone began to vibrate soon as we made it through the front door. I pulled it out and slumped into the couch kickin' my shoes off.

Sunni headed straight for the bedroom already on her phone and Babygirl went to hers. It was afta 3:30 and I knew they was tired. I had a recent text from Ms. D letting me know Rudy called and giving me his number, and asking what I wanted her to do bout Red. He just coming down to help.

Well, get him situated when he gets here, I replied, and set my phone down. I grabbed it and sent Rudy a quick text letting him know it's me, and ta come ta LA Fitness June 1st in Lil Rock.

I sent Lance the same message. I needed ta hurry and find me a building to set up shop and fast, then I could worry bout putting some of the Dream Team on the road and doing parties and shit. I leaned my head back and considered my next move.

—•—

I must've fallen asleep because I woke up to Sunni telling me to come eat. She'd made a three cheese spaghetti with Texas toast garlic bread. I got up and made my way to the kitchen. Babygirl was already at the table, and I looked at the wall clock and it was just now turning 6.

"Babygirl, Daddy got sum'n to tell you," I told her. She just stared at me. "Well, you know Sunni's pregnant. Do you want a sister or a brother?" I asked.

She was so happy she didn't know how to answer.

"Ummm...I'd like a brother, so it can be two boys and two girls," she replied.

"That'll be straight wit me too," I said, and with that we sat down and ate as a family.

After dinner I was in for the night. I got me a shower and laid on down. Sunni cleaned up the kitchen and then came in to lay down beside me.

She cuddled up into my chest and I reached across her and grabbed her phone.

"Hey what's your password ma?" I asked, looking at the lock screen. I didn't remember seeing one on her phone before.

Sunni's head shot up. "Why?" she asked quickly.

I kept hold of her phone as she squirmed against me. "I was gonna look into some similar businesses to see what they got going on on their websites. I'm thinking of asking Shonequa to set one up for me."

Sunni slipped her phone out of my hand and turned it away, punching in a pass code quick. That got me boiling but before I could say anything she asked, "Why you don't want Ms. D and the girls to handle that for you?"

"Well they did set up the company's Facebook," I said as she snuggled back in under my arm, "and they have a good handle on social media. But I want to diversify. I don't like putting all my eggs in one basket, you know?"

Sunni nodded.

"That's a good idea E. I know you get along with them all and you're trying to do your bro a favor keeping his crew in cash, but I don't think it's a good idea to tie yourself to him."

"I agree," I said, and although I felt a little guilty saying it out loud, she was right. Lil Jon might be behind bars for now but there was something about how Ms. D was acting that had me fucked up.

At first I thought we were just hooking up, but now it seemed more and more like she was trying to seduce me, especially with how she had Kim backing her schemes up.

Hopefully mentioning that Sunni was pregnant would make her back off. I had seen her face and she was freaked out. The last thing I needed was another woman coming after me while I was trying to settle down with my family and get this business and cash secure.

My eyes were getting heavy and Sunni had started to breathe deep and easy. I followed her to sleep quickly.

—•—

The week flew by and Sunday rolled around quick. I'd been so busy that the weekend came fast. I rolled outta bed and it was hitting 7 AM. I got myself together and went to the living room to call Kay.

"Mmmm...Hello?" Kay answered the phone still in sleep mode.

"Getcha ass up! We got a lot to do today and we going to see Lil Jon," I told her.

"Mmmk," she said and hung up.

I grabbed another shower and got dressed in something cool. Some jean shorts, a v-neck, and some all black Airmax. I had to hit the mall and get my shoe game up soon as I got straight.

Sunni and Babygirl were up getting ready for church. I kissed them bye and headed out. At 8:30 in the morning it was already hot as hell. Jumpin in my BMW, I dropped the sunroof and headed to Kay's.

I pulled up at Kay's and she was outside talking to her neighbor waiting on me. She hugged her friend and jumped in the passenger seat.

"Hey bro. Damn, you got a bitch up early in the morning!" she said, fixing her hair in the mirror.

"We gotta go see bro, then you can get back to ya sleep," I told her, heading to the county jail.

"Hey," I said after a few minutes of silence, "can I ask you a question sis?"

Kay gave me side-eye. "You know you can," she said.

"I jus wanted to run something by you. You know I love Sunni, and I'm planning on asking her to marry me soon." Kay sat up excitedly and I held my hand up to keep her quiet. "She's been acting not herself lately," I continued, thinking back to the passcode on Sunni's phone and how she hadn't given it to me yet.

"Well she is pregnant," Kay said.

"That's not what I mean. She's tired most of the time yeah and moody, but all of a sudden she's got a passcode on her phone. And I been seeing some texts come through from numbers I don't recognize."

"Just numbers?" Kay asked, glancing at me. "No name for a contact or anything?"

I shook my head.

"What kinda stuff do the texts say?"

"Nothing specific or suspicious really. I just been away so long I don't know what's normal for women anymore, you know sis? I want to think she's loyal, and she's definitely been supporting me through everything, but something seems off."

Kay was frowning now looking out the window as we headed down the highway.

"I'm not gonna lie, bro, that does sound a little suspicious.

But all I've seen personally is Sunni being there to back you up in this business and being a mom to your Babygirl when she needs it."

I felt myself starting to calm down.

"She has been great with Babygirl," I agreed.

Kay nodded. "And she'll be great with the new life you two are creating, too. Just give her some space. Sometimes women don't like to feel like they being watched all the time. She needs her own life too E."

I settled down, mulling over what Kay had said. I loved having Sunni back me up and want to play a part in getting this business going, but Kay was right. It would be good to give Sunni some personal space and let her have her friends.

Pulling up outside the prison, the parking lot wasn't too packed. But it had a nice little line when we made it through the door.

They checked us over and gave us the list of rules. No putting our hands under the tables, no trying to pass things, ask the guards if we needed anything. It was weird to be on the other side of things but it felt good to know I wouldn't be coming back here any time soon. Once it had been Lil Jon visiting me like this right after I had first got put away.

When Lil Jon came out Kay started crying. Looking at lil bro behind that glass damn near brought tears to my eyes. He smiled real big when he seen me and Kay. I picked up the receiver on my side as Lil Jon did the same on his.

"Wassup lil bro? How you holding up?" I asked.

"Man, I'm good but ready to get da fuck outta here. My lawyer said we don't have a self-defense law down here, but can get me on it," he replied.

"Awrighty, did you have any dope on you?"

"Nope, just some money and a lil smoke sack. That's not a felony. I was going to buy some pills and the nigga tried to rob me," he replied. "But I had already sold all my product and was going to stock up the week after. Lucky I guess."

We talked about the house and my business and I asked was his books straight, and apparently Ms. D been on her shit. I still dropped another $300 on his books anyway.

"Hey listen E," Lil Jon said, hunkering down and looking right at me. "Ms. D been keeping me up to date on your business. It sounds like you all are bringing in the cash. I know she offered to help you out with storing all that money and she said you turned her down."

Kay gave me a look like she wasn't getting involved in this.

I recognized Lil Jon's tone of voice; he still thought he was the boss, despite being the one behind the glass.

"Yeah, I turned her down," I said, pulling my own chair up to the glass. "Listen I appreciate your crew helping me out, and I want to make sure your property and people are taken care of Lil Jon, but I'm not getting involved in any bullshit anymore."

"Did I ask you to start moving product?" Jon asked in a hard voice.

"No," I said, "but that doesn't mean you aren't planning on getting some shit started from in here. Ms. D was right in what she told you — everything I'm doing is taking off, and I'm not going to let anything stop me. I'm happy to give your crew a little work so that everything is still ready to go when you're out, but my business will not be tied to you or yours in any way."

I couldn't make it more clear, and I could tell that Lil Jon wasn't happy. His face was stone hard. Back in the day I might have backed down — that's how he got me working in the dope game in the first place, that and the fast money — but now I had a family to take care of.

"I'll let you two talk," I said, standing up and squeezing Kay's shoulder quick. She looked uncomfortable but relieved that she didn't need to get involved.

I went out to my car. I sat in the car with the air on and fifteen minutes later Kay came out smiling in a better mood.

"I see you aight now," I said as she got in the car.

"Yeah, I'm straight now. He'll be out soon," she said.

"That's good," I said. "But I was serious about everything I said Kay. I'm not letting him get a grip on my business. I told you when I got out that I was going to do right by you and Babygirl, and I am."

Kay smiled at me with tears in her eyes. "That's good to hear bro. You know I love Lil Jon but I don't want to see you back behind that glass again. But what are you going to do now? He's getting out soon and you don't have a building yet for the business."

"We gonna use the house to host private parties," I said decisively. I had been thinking about it but now that the pressure was on, I know we'd have to have a place to work out of to bring money in quick, and Lil Jon's place was perfect for it. Ms. D wouldn't argue with me because she was a greedy bitch and knew it would bring in the money.

"But I'm still gonna open up a club," I told her as we headed back North Little Rock to Lil Jon's spot. "Doing one show at the house a week, open to the public, should give me enough to get a down payment on a building. Do you wanna help me find a place?" I asked.

Kay bounced excitedly. "I would love to!" she exclaimed. "I already got some ideas. I'll get atchu as soon as I find a few spots that look good. Just keep getting that money, E."

Pulling up at Ms. D's spot, the only car in the driveway was hers. I told Kay I'd be back and went to see what was up with Lil Jon's stuff. When I walked in the house D was on the couch watching TV.

"Wassup E?" she said when she looked up at me.

"Not shit ma, just stopped by to get Jon's shit. You aight?" I asked.

"Yeah I'm good. How he doing anyway?" she asked.

"Aww shit bro straight. He got bigga and his lawyer told him to sit back. So shit sound straight right now."

"Cool. I meant to tell ya, I had packed his stuff already and put everything in a U-Haul storage," she said.

"Aight bet, that'll save me some time. Preciate it," I replied. Then my phone began to vibrate. I looked at the screen and it was Sunni.

"I'ma get back at you lata ma," I told her and headed back out the door to my car. "Hey bae, I just bout to call you," I said, answering the call.

"Oh really? Why didn't you text me back? Where you at anyways?" Sunni asked.

"Droppin Kay off now and on my way back to the house," I told her.

"Okay, I'll meet you there. Freshen up, you know we gotta be at my momma's in like an hour and a half."

"Okay bae, I gotchu, calm down," I replied. I gave her my love and hung up.

"She just moody, but you gotta be patient with her too," Kay said as we rolled through the Lil Rock streets. I nodded and just turned up the music and bobbed my head. At some point I would have to tell Ms. D what I had planned for Lil Jon's spot.

—•—

By the time I pulled up back in Dumas, Sunni was parked on the street, sitting in the A/C in her car. I honked at her and parked before jumping in her passenger seat.

"Where Babygirl at bae?" I asked, looking in the back seat.

"She already at momma's and we're late!" she said with a small attitude.

"I'm sorry bae, you know I had to go handle that shit with my lil brother," I replied.

Sunni calmed down at the mention of Lil Jon. "I know. How's he doing anyways? And where'd you get that ring?"

"Aw, this bro shit. D already had his shit packed and put up by the time I got there. She gave me an extra key to the U-Haul where it's stored," I told her and then I realized we were pulling up at this nice ass house on the other side of town.

"Damn! Ya folks got a nice house," I told her.

"Yeah, I know," she replied. I was kinda nervous about her parents, especially her dad. Didn't really know how he was gonna take to me or my occupation, but we gotta get it over with sooner rather than later. I sprayed on a little squirt of my Polo Red that I left in her car and we headed inside.

—•—

After we finished dinner, we sat and talked to her parents, Lance Jr., and Nikki before we went home. I still hadn't told anyone about her being pregnant and that I planned on proposing to her. I got to meet Nikki's kids Shalondon and Karis. I laid Babygirl down and went back to the living room with Sunni.

After a long day in the heat she still looked like a real goddess.

"Bae, my parents took to you really well. Especially my dad," she said as I stretched out on the couch and laid my head in her lap.

"Yeah, I thought ya pops was gonna give me a case bout my job, but he seemed to be straight with it."

"Yeah, he's not a bad person. He respects that you're doing your thing and you're a business man," she said.

"Right now it's time to get some rest because I got a long day tomorrow," I told her, and we headed toward the bedroom. I kicked off my shoes, put on some shorts and a v-neck and laid down with the tablet while Sunni surfed through TV channels. I got online and had a boatload of requests from dudes wanting to be part of the team. I looked through em and added a few, sent em my info to call. I finished that and called Shonequa bout the magazine and pictures.

When I got off the phone Sunni reminded me of the doctor's appointment at 9 AM. I looked at the time and it was after 10. Ms. D sent me a text saying: *Gave ya bro ya numba. Gotta talk to you he said.*

I just replied "Okay," and laid back on the pillow cuddled up to my bae. I closed my eyes and drifted through my thoughts until I fell asleep.

10

Raheem

I ENJOYED THE DAY WITH Diamond and we were getting real close. Keisha finally stopped calling, but still popped up at the clubs and shit where I be at. The girl was crazy, but she was also a dead weight too.

The toilet flushed, bringing me out of my thoughts, and Diamond walked out wearing white lace booty shorts and no bra. She had some pretty ass titties like forreal.

"You got a nice pad, Papi," she said, climbing on top of me and placing kisses on my chiseled chest. She had spent all morning asking me questions about my job and E's plans for the business. I had tried to be evasive and keep a lot to myself, but it was hard when she was lovin up on me like she was.

"Yeah, I gotta keep my spot clean," I replied.

"I see, but I've been wanting to holla atchu bout something," she said.

"Wassup ma?" I asked, rolling her over and laying her on her back beside me.

"I don't mean to get in yo B.I Papi, but I overheard you talking to ya boy Gee in the club bout the bread ya'll was generating from doing shows, and how ya boss needed to get a building. Well I got a solution to your problem," she said, looking up at me and waiting on my response.

"Whatchu got in mind babe?" I asked, a little suspicious. I liked the woman but I didn't think it was a good idea to mix business and pleasure.

"Well me and my girls been to a few of your shows before we met, and as you know I'ma business woman. I got a building ya'll could use and do ya thing at. It's already set up with tables and chairs and all the accessories," she said, taking a breath.

As soon as she said that I got excited, but tried to keep my cool. If we could find a spot to get things really going we'd be bringing in way more cash than we were now doing house calls.

"Yeah, I preciate that bae, but that's not my call," I said, leaning back. "I'ma have to holla at E bout that."

"Okay, do that. Or betta yet set it up for us to meet tomorrow if he's not too busy."

"Alright. I can do that in the morning. But in the meantime…" and with that said I laid that dick game down on her, and we fell asleep tangled up in each other's arms.

Big E

Sunni woke me up early Monday morning to a light breakfast in bed. She was already dressed. I ate, hit the shower, and dressed for the cool weather today. It was cloudy and about 70 degrees so I threw on a Polo collar shirt, Ralph Lauren jeans, and a pair of retro Jordan's Sunni got for me a few weeks ago.

I went to the living room where the girls were at. Sunni

was doing Babygirl's hair, watching the news.

I gave Babygirl $20 for the day, gave her and Sunni both kisses on the forehead, and headed out the front door. I peeped at my phone which had a 70% battery life left.

I had a message from my nigga Gee and one from my nigga Raheem. I called Gee first to see what was poppin wit him.

"What's good boss man?" he said, answering the phone.

"Just got your message, wassup with you?" I asked.

"Jus checking in, haven't heard from you in a day or two. How's everything going?" he asked.

"Aww shit looking up. I was gonna run shit outta Lil Jon spot, but I gotta keep it professional, so I'ma go ahead and count up and see what we got jumpin."

"Bet. Let me know what I need ta do. It's about time," he joked.

"You know you my right hand so you're in the mix with me, but I gotchu," I replied, and disconnected the call. Gee really was one of few people I trusted in this game. I looked at my other message from Raheem.

Got a business proposition for you, can we meet up lata?

I replied, *I'll text you when I'm free.* I liked Raheem but it made me nervous when young guns tried to get involved in business to quick. They had their own ideas and I'd been planning this business for years. I'd have to hear him out but be sure to make it clear who the boss was.

I hit my sunroof and let the windows down and backed out the driveway bumpin the "Carter 4" by Weezy and headed to North Little Rock to Shonequa's spot. I texted her to let her know I was on my way.

I hit the one way rushing, like Future said.

—•—

I pulled up at Shonequa's in Lakewood Village and I really wanted to get me a house out here, but I didn't know yet. Just another reason I was feeling the pressure to find a permanent home for Hard Bodies.

I parked behind her car and made my way to the front door. She opened it before I could knock.

"Hey Evan!" she said excitedly.

"Damn, somebody's in a good mood," I replied.

"Yeah, well we had a good meeting last time, but everything's good, just ready to get your magazine started."

"Well let's get to work."

After I finished giving her my story line, we went through some photos online and she picked out some that she wanted to use. But we still had a lotta work to do before my first magazines got published. She wanted me to send the men over there two at a time. So we set that up too.

"Can I ask you another question Miss Shonequa?" I asked, reclining on her couch.

"Of course," she said with a coy smile.

"So I'm looking to branch out from the crew I have handling things now. You've been doing such a great job with the magazine that I was wondering if you would like to help us out with setting up the company website, or if you have any good recommendations," I said.

Shonequa leaned forward thoughtfully. "I could probably handle that for you," she said. "We'd have to meet again to go over what you have in mind for the website, but I definitely think we could use some of these photos and this info for it. I'll get atchu when I'm free and let you know what else I'll need from you to get it up and running."

"That's what I like to hear," I said, grinning and clapping my hands. "Stick with me ma and you can have a permanent place in this business."

She laughed and I was hit once again by how gorgeous she was. "I believe you Evan, just looking at how quickly everything is coming together for you, I definitely think you're going to be a success. I'd be happy to be on your team."

She leaned forward and we shook hands.

I told her I'd be in touch, I wanted to tap that ass again. She had a pair of them blue jean daisy dukes, ankle socks, and a muscle shirt. I shook it off, gave her a hug, and headed to Ms. D's spot to check on the fellas because she had em all over there checking out their progress.

My phone vibrated before I got in the car. It was my guy Rudy. I just told him to meet me at D's house and gave him the directions.

I headed to Ms. D's, and it was just now going on 10. I texted Sunni, she said the baby was fine and I told her so was my interview, and I'd see her in a minute.

———•—

Pulling up at Ms. D's I seen Raheem's Chevy, BG's Delta, Gee's Denali, and AB's Crown Vic. I walked in the house. Music was playing and laughs were being shared. In the family room and everyone was sitting around kicking it and talking amongst themselves. Ms. D looked up first.

"Wassup dude, finally you decide to show up. Ya boy Red need somebody to come get him from the airport," she said.

"Bet, I'ma have Kay swing down on him on her way over here," I told her, walking right by her. I could tell she had an attitude that I wasn't paying attention to her but I was done playing her games. It was time to get serious.

I texted Kay before I sat down next to Sunni. My nigga Gee look like he was enjoying this, but I was bout to retire my nigga since we were hiring some new help.

Then I noticed the Mexican looking chick sitting by Raheem, Kim, and Tana. Looking her over quickly I recognized her as a dangerous woman. She looked like she could handle herself, and I wasn't sure what she was doing here. She was probably walking all over Heem and I couldn't have that if he was going to be involved with the business.

I told Heem to follow me to the back office.

"What you need to holla at me bout lil bruh?" I asked, deciding to ask him about his woman after.

"Aww, well I'ma get my girl explain it, but E lemme tell you this. This girl got paper." He was rubbing his hands together, and I knew he was excited. Powerful women were always tempting but you had to be careful with them. He was too young to see that yet.

"That night I broke bread with you, that was change she gave me," he continued.

"Okay, let me get this straight. Your girl wanna do B.I. with me. I'ma check out her game and see if she talking proper. Tell her and Sunni to come back here," I told him and he left to go get the women.

I sat in the chair behind the desk and twiddled my thumbs until Sunni came in first, then Heem's girl, followed by him and he closed the door.

"What's good ma? My name's Evan but they call me Big E. This my girl Shaneka, but we call her Sunni, and I'm sure you've met everyone else," I said.

"Yeah I have, and thanks for agreeing to give me a lil bit of your time," she replied, and she was professional right away. Heem was in deep, he was staring at her like he was in love.

"My name's Sasha but everyone calls me Diamond. I overheard your guys talking about ya'll needing a building to open up your club, and I just so happen to buy a building with a stage, tables, and bar," she continued.

Heem frowned at that and I knew she must not be telling the whole truth there.

"You just happened to overhear that we need a building?" I asked bluntly.

Diamond didn't even break a sweat, she just kept smiling at me. "Yeah. I been around you and your boys for a while, went to a few house parties where they came to play."

That was plausible, but I'd have to talk to the guys later about keeping their mouths shut around the clientele.

"So what's in it for you?" I asked. "I mean, I already got one business partner and I know this just ain't fall in a nigga lap..."

"Bae just hear her out!" Sunni said, cutting me off. It seemed that in the time they'd been left alone in the living room, they'd made fast friends. Sunni clearly liked Diamond.

"I just require a small percentage and me and my girls get VIP every time we touch down. You can also rent the place for bachelorette parties and such. It can be a male strip club and some," Diamond stated. She seemed very comfortable pitching me this information and I wondered how long she had been sitting on this for.

I sat there for a minute before asking, "How much of a percentage are we talking?"

Even though I was a little worried about this woman stepping up so quickly and strongly, she had me. I needed a place to put down roots and get the guys on regular shows. And if I could avoid using Lil Jon's place at all, that would be ideal.

"Hmmm. I'm not a picky girl, I got money, I'm just tryna do a favor for my papi-thulo. And you've come up with something that's going to radiate some bread in the south. So I'd say 20%," she said.

"Damn, I already gave D 20%, that'll push me down to –"

"Babe, stop being greedy. 20% ain't shit, you'll still be making your ends," Sunni cut me off again. That pissed me off, but she was right. This is a huge burden lifted off my shoulders.

"Aight ma, I gotchu. I'll be in touch with you to see this building," I told Diamond, and stood up.

"That's what's up. I'll have my lawyer type up a business agreement and can't wait to get this money with you," Diamond said, standing and shaking my hand before her and Raheem left. I had to admit, this woman had an ass that had Sunni's eyes glued to it. I just chucked to myself.

"What's so funny?" Sunni asked.

"That's what you would call a royal ass. Don't get me wrong bae, you're thick, but that's a Clydesdale!" I replied, and we both busted out laughing as we headed back to the family room.

"I got good news for everyone. The game just changed for us," I said, drawing everyone's attention.

"Wassup E?" Gee asked.

"Well as ya'll know we've been doing house calls, now everyone's gonna be able to show up to see you fellas live and in person. You all have met Raheem's lady friend Ms. Diamond. Well apparently she owns a lil real estate and has offered me a building that's already equipped with everything –"

"Oh did she now?" Ms. D said, cutting me off. I expected this from her. She'd been feeling some kinda way since I told her Sunni was pregnant, and my visit with Lil Jon had her nervous. He probably called her and told her I wasn't getting involved with them further.

"Yeah, and this is an opportunity for us to get this started. I'ma go check the place out and get it inspected and ready for opening," I finished.

"Time to get this money," Gee said.

"And you fellas gotta do interviews for the magazine this week, so keep ya phones on and scheduled open. BG and Gee will go tomorrow, Raheem and Sam Wednesday, and AB you and Steph will go Thursday. We gonna throw a lil party this weekend to celebrate the come up," I said and everyone got to cheering and clapping.

"Umm, we could celebrate at my place, I got an in-ground pool and pool table and small bar with a grill on my patio. We can kick it pool side," Diamond said, and the cheering got louder.

I don't know where Raheem got this woman from, but he had him something. It was something bout her though that seemed kinda suspicious and dangerous. I was gonna keep my eye on her.

Then came a knock on the door. I went to get it as Sunni sat down by Kim and Tana and they began to chat. I was happy as long as she approved of the moves I was making, as long as a nigga didn't have to deal with the dope game, I was straight. But everything was about to make a complete turnaround.

I opened the door and my nigga Rudy stood there.

"Wassup fam, come in! I see you found the place okay," I told him.

"Yeah, I got here alright. Ya'll having a party of what?"

"Nah, just a business meeting," I told him. I took him where everyone was and introduced him to everybody and told Gee to look out for bro. I wanted to go grab a bite to eat. I kissed Sunni before leaving out, jumping in the BMW and heading toward Protho Junction to KFC.

My phone went off, it was a text from Kay with her letting me know that she went and picked Red up but his flight was late. So everything was looking up so far and I couldn't wait to get this off the ground.

—•—

After picking up some chicken and sides I pulled back up to D's house. The heat was starting to pick up. I rolled my windows up, grabbed the bags, and headed in the house and shit was still jumpin but my youn'n Raheem and Diamond had already headed out.

I'm guessing since business was handled he knew wassup and they had no need to stick around. My nigga Rudy was choppin game with Ms. D when I walked in.

I sat the bucket of chicken down with a roll of paper towels and told everybody I'd be back, I had to place a few calls.

Instead of putting Red up at Ms. D's I decided to find him an apartment while he was down here. I wanted to get as far away from Lil Jon's shit as I could. But Ms. D had been hitting me up constantly even though I didn't answer her — she was definitely nervous now that I was making ties with other business partners.

I went into the back room where we conduct our B.I. and searched the net for an apartment and found one at Protho Manor, which was up the street.

I called the manager named Fred and told him I needed a three bedroom and I'd be paid up for 6 months. My phone vibrated as soon as I hung up and it was a number I didn't recognize. I ignored it first, then it called again, so I answered.

A robotic voice told me it was Lil Jon. I accepted the call.

"Wassup lil bro?" I asked, excited to hear from him. He gave me the rundown about the shit his lawyer talking and so far so good.

I gave him the rundown on my end and he was happy to hear I finally got a building set up and we'd be opening it up soon. I told him I'd send Ms. D to see him tomorrow and to keep his head up.

After I hung up I made my way back to the family room. Kay sent me a text saying he'd be landing in a few. I sat next to

Sunni. She had an appointment for next month a couple days before my birthday.

I told her I had some shit to handle and I'd be back to get her. I grabbed me a couple pieces of chicken and paper towels for the road and headed out. At the U-Haul storage unit I looked through some of Lil Jon's shit. Lil bro had a lotta expensive shit, especially his jewelry. I locked it all back up and headed to the house for a split lil second to stash bro's jewelry up in a safe.

—•—

When I pulled up Lance Jr. was in the driveway. I parked Sunni's Q50 behind him and got out, throwing the paper towel away on the side of the house.

"Wassup nigga?" I asked.

"Man, not too much of shit. Just wanted to stop by and check on my sister. Where she at?"

"In North Little Rock at my homegirl house. You wanna ride out there wit me?" I asked him.

"Yeah let's ride bro." We jumped in the Infiniti and headed back to North Little Rock, stopping at Taylor's Law Firm to holla at a nigga named Wayne about my brother, and getting me a lawyer for my club.

Me and Lance made small talk as he fired up that gas. I rolled the windows down as we puffed down, talking bout what's to come with this male stripper shit.

My phone vibrated loud in the cup holder.

"Speak!" I answered.

"Wassup E?" the voice said.

"Who dis?"

"JD."

"Aww shit, wassup bro?"

"Not shit, at my gram's house," he replied.

"Gimme a minute I'ma be through there," I told him and hung up.

"Who dat?" Lance asked.

"My nigga," I said, and hit the blunt before passing it back.

When I rolled through Rose City, ain't too much of shit changed. Mu'fuckas was doing they thang, niggas be grillin outside, kids playing ball on the broke down basketball court, while mommas, sisters, or aunts sat gossiping. I pulled up to JD's spot and hit the horn twice.

A few minutes later this big yella ass nigga come out. The boy got big as hell. He jumped in behind me.

"Wassup big bro, it's been a minute," he said, happy to see me.

"Yeah it has, but peep this — we got a lot riding on this stripper B.I. so I need you to stay on your game. This here is Lance Jr, head of Security. He'll make sho everybody straight and since you on parole, I'ma have you with the Arkansas team," I told him.

"That's wassup big bro, just let me know wassup," he replied. I gave my nigga some dap as he jumped out and headed back in his house. We headed back to Ms. D's to see what they had jumpin.

—●—

We pulled up and I noticed a few more cars had left. We hopped out and headed inside. I looked at my phone, it was nearing 3:30 in the afternoon. Sunni jumped up when she seen Lance Jr. She hugged and kissed me, then jumped on her brotha.

"E, it looks like you real gotcha shit together with this stripper shit," he said, putting Sunni back on her feet.

"Yeah man, I'ma go check the building out tomorrow or lata this week."

"Aww you got a spot now, huh?" he asked.

"Yeah and it come with a bitness partner, but it came cheap. I'ma take my time, but gotta open it as soon as possible if I wanna keep the team on my side," I told him.

"You right bout that."

"But my nigga there's chicken and plates on the table, dig in fam," I told Lance Jr. I felt like this shit couldn't get any better. Lance made him a plate and set beside Tana.

"Are you okay?" I asked Sunni.

"All this excitement has a bitch tired," she replied.

"Well lemme take you home then." I motioned for Lance Jr. and told him what the deal was and we headed back home. It was hot now, so it was time for her to get her a nap. Babygirl was at her friends and I didn't have to worry about getting her til later.

—·—

After I got settled in and Sunni dozed off instantly. I went back in the living room with Lance, but he'd already left.

My phone vibrated in my pocket. Now this was the worst thing about starting a business, the phone never stopped ringing.

This time it was just a text from Ms. D saying Shonequa's been looking for me. I gave her a call and she just wanted to knock shit out in one day. She told me to give her a couple days, which was fine with me.

I sent Gee a text to let the guys know about the change. I was sitting and thinkin of the show Ms. D told me bout. My ex — Tara's birthday was coming up and she wanted us. I called my nigga Cornell to see if he was busy.

He said he was free, so I booked him for the whole weekend. We were gonna do Tara's party Friday and our celebration party Saturday night.

In between my thoughts, Babygirl came running in.

"What'd you do today lil girl?" I asked, tugging on her braids.

"Went to the Boys and Girls Club."

"That sounds fun. Now get you a shower and get ready to settle in for the night," I told her, and she sprang for her room.

It was almost 7 o'clock. I figured Babygirl had ate while she was out, so I didn't have to cook or order nothing. I was also in the process of ordering a Mercedes van to transport the guys to and from the airport or local shows and house calls.

A few minutes later the doorbell rang. "Come in," I shouted, and Gee opened the door.

"Wassup fam?" I asked when he came in.

"Not shit, just came to see what you had poppin."

"Not shit, let's take a ride." It was getting late, but shit, I had to tie up the rest of these ends. With the van, buying an apartment, and everything else funds was getting low. I had a lil over 40K in the safe so I had to be careful with the money now.

"Let's ride fam," I told Gee and we went and jumped in his Denali. Babygirl went straight to sleep after her shower, so the house was down.

11

Big E

WE PULLED UP TO THE dealership to check out this van at Steve Lander's on University in Little Rock and I was paying cash for a 2013 Mercedes Van that had rims.

"My guy Red jus arrived, so we gonna drop the van off at Ms. D's, pick him up, and go pay the 6 month lease on that apartment."

We jumped out and Mr. Landers met us at the door. "Thanks for agreeing to stay open for me," I said, shaking his hand.

"Nonsense! Any friend of Jon's is a friend of mine. Give Jon my prayers. But here's the van you're looking for," he said, pointing to a white van.

"So how much?" I asked because all I brought was ten bands with me.

"For you I'll let it go for 8K, and it's fully loaded," he replied.

The price was high but I wasn't bout to let em take me fast.

"Man, I can do 5. That's high for a van over 100 thousand miles."

"I'll go 7500," he replied.

"Can you do 6 then, because a brother on his last leg," I told him.

"Yeah I guess we can do 6, only if you agree to shop with me again," he said.

"That's something I will do," I told him, and we headed inside to sign the papers.

—•—

Driving the van back to Ms. D's, it rode smooth and had a nice sound system. I pulled up beating in the neighborhood. Some of the lights were on in the house. I chopped game with Red and introduced Kim and Gee.

He'd already met Ms. D and her girls. I'd introduce him to the rest later. It was getting late and I wanted to remind Ms. D to get with Cornell and see what everything looking like.

Gee dropped me off and we headed out.

—•—

At home the girls were still asleep, so I brushed my teeth, washed my face and hit the bed. It was past 10 and I was tired, but the rest of this week was straight business. It was only the beginning....

Made in the USA
Middletown, DE
06 April 2021

36927267R00128